Still Scheming

By: Y'vet

METROPOLITAN COLLEGE OF NY
LIBRARY, 12TH FLOOR
431 CANAL STREET
NEW YORK, NY 10013

Chapter 1

"Rena get down! They're right behind you!" Chandelle warned as Slim and his boy ran down the alley a foot away from snatching Rena by the collar.

Slim snatched his gun from his waistband and slammed it across the back of Rena's head causing her to fall to the ground bleeding from the gash just behind her left ear.

"Rena! Rena!" Chandelle screamed as she continued running down the moonlit alley. Chandelle was only a yard away from the lighted street. A group of partygoers were just leaving the bar allowing her a chance to get lost in the crowd and lessen the opportunity of being shot in front of witnesses.

"Go 'head and run baby but you'll be back to get your girl or she's dead. Bring my shit and ya'll might live." Slim yelled after Chandelle as she disappeared in the crowd. "Grab that bitch up Rome and throw her ass in the truck. Let's get the fuck out of here before anyone sees us."

****

The jury walked into the courtroom passing the concealed envelope to the bailiff. Walking

towards the bench the bailiff passed the verdict to the judge.

Slowly, the judge opened the envelope reading the contents and nodded. Judge Watkins faced the jury and spoke,

"Have you all agreed on the verdict?"

"Yes your honor." The jury spoke in unison.

"You may all be seated." The jury took their seats and looked at the defendant waiting for the verdict to be read.

"Will the defendant please rise? On the charges of murder in the first degree, burglary, possession of a firearm, and criminal negligence, the jury finds the defendant Chandelle Carter guilty. The Commonwealth of Pennsylvania sentences you to twenty-five years to life in a high security women's correctional facility without the chance of parole." The judge banged his gavel signifying the final decision. Chandelle began screaming and crying uncontrollably. Immediately she was handcuffed and led to the doors and down the hallway to the passageway towards the prison. *"Please! Please! I'm sorry! I didn't mean to do it! I didn't mean to do it! Please believe me!"* Chandelle screamed hoping to have another chance to convince the jury of her sincerity.

"Miss? Miss? Are you alright? Is there anything I can get you?"

Chandelle opened her eyes realizing that for the third day straight she had been having the same recurring dream. Embarrassed, Chandelle reached for her purse to straightened her hair and fix her makeup. Clearing her throat and apologizing to the stewardess she said,

"Um, Yes, I'm fine. No, I don't need anything. I just had a bad dream." She looked in the mirror and realized she didn't look half as bad as she felt. Wanting the stewardess to walk away and lose the unwanted attention she was getting from the other passengers, she asked the stewardess to bring her a bottle of water and a cup of ice.

I can't take too much more of this shit! I should be happy and excited because everything I ever wanted is about to come true. I have a couple of million dollars put away in an off-shore account in the islands and I never have to worry about money again. My friends are safe and financially secure and the police don't have a clue about what I did or how I did it. The best thing that came from all this is that crazy bitch Angela is dead and I don't ever have to worry about her sorry ass again. My only regret is that I don't have Derrick here to share my life with .Oh well... Men are a dime a dozen. If I had to make the same choices today I wouldn't change a thing. There's nothin' I hate more than a weak ass man! Love would've had my ass caught up and probably in jail trying to take him and his feelings in consideration. I watched enough movies and read enough books to know that love does nothin' but get your ass hemmed up. There'll be another Derrick if love is meant to be. I just pray that once I get to the island and get comfortable in my surroundings, these damn dreams will go away. I think I'm just worried about leaving Rena behind until she gets another passport to join me. I still don't know how that girl lost her passport at the last minute. I'll have to call her as soon as I get settled.

"Here's your water. Is there anything else I can get for you?" Recognizing the stewardess had returned, Chandelle thanked her.

"How long until we land?"

"We'll be landing in the next thirty minutes. You can flag me or one of the other stewardesses and we will be happy to collect your trash when you're finished."

"Thank you so much." Chandelle checked her carry-on baggage under her seat and grabbed her planner from the side pocket. *I'll get to St. Croix around six o'clock in the evening so getting to the bank tonight is out of the question. I'll grab a taxi at the airport and get a hotel room for the night. Maybe, there'll be a decent bar nearby where I can unwind, have a couple of those island drinks and take in the scenery. Tomorrow I have an appointment with the banker at nine and that should give me enough time to meet the real estate agent by eleven. Ms. Carlisle said she had a couple of properties to show me. I hope she understands what I'm looking for cause I definitely don't want to spend more than a week in a hotel room. I shoulda sent her a couple of pictures from a magazine to be sure. I half understood a damn word coming from her mouth. The dialect here is gonna kick my ass. I can see that now. One thing's for sure, I won't have problems counting my money in my bank account though. Maybe I'll get done early enough so that I can get some shopping done I really need to buy some clothes. I don't know why I didn't think to buy appropriate clothing when I planned to move here.*

Chandelle heard the captain announce that they were making their approach and asked that the passengers return their trays to an upright position and fasten their seatbelts to prepare for landing.

****

At seven thirty that evening Chandelle entered her room at the St. Croix Plaza Hotel.

Oh My Gosh! This place is absolutely gorgeous! Chandelle walked over to the balcony pulling back the drapes, opening the French doors leading to the veranda.

I bet the sunset is lovely from here and the beach and water is beautiful. I need to get a shower and get dressed. I'm tired as hell but I'll be damned if I miss out on my first night of soaking in all of this beauty.

Chandelle decided to put on her yellow strapless dress with the matching four-inch strappy heels she got on sale at Macys. It complimented her honey brown skin and her freshly cut bob hairstyle. Looking in the mirror she had to admit that she looked good.

I'm loving these golden highlights in my hair. I'm so glad I let Debra put them in. I really needed a change of pace. Now if I can only lose a couple of pounds I'll be happy. Chandelle primped in the mirror checking out all angles. Her new size twelve was starting to grow on her. She caught two brothas' checkin' her out when she was in the airport retrieving her luggage. *Damn my ass and thighs are thick. Well, I ain't runnin' out here buyin' no car anytime soon so maybe I can lose some of this weight walking around the island. But on second thought, if I lose it cool and if I don't that's okay too. I must admit though I do look damn good.* Chandelle put the finishing touches on her makeup and was out the door within the hour.

****

Chandelle found a lovely outdoor café close to the water Sipping a Mai Tai garnished with mint and lime slices,

Chandelle was grooving to a Caribbean beat that had her wanting to get up and shake her behind.

"You seem to be enjoying yourself Miss Lady. Mind if I join you? Chandelle swiveled in her chair to face the voice whispering in her ear. She nodded fearing the words that would come out of her mouth.

"Can I buy you another of whatever you're having?" Again she nodded. Her mind was willing her to speak but she couldn't force the words to pass her lips. Chandelle was mesmerized by the figure now sitting next to her. She figured he had to be over six feet tall with the most hypnotic eyes she had ever seen. Skin the color of a tootsie roll and locks that hung past his shoulders. *Damn I wouldn't mind unwrapping his package and tasting his sweetness.* Listening to his accent she wasn't sure if he was native to the island but guessed he was or lived in St. Croix for a long time.

"Thank you so much. I have a really busy day planned for tomorrow. I'm gonna have to watch how many of these things I drink."

"So, the beautiful lady speaks. I thought maybe you didn't really want to be bothered for a minute there." Chandelle blushed at the compliment.

"It's my first night here on the island. You startled me but I welcome the company."

"Now I guess it's my turn to blush." He said lifting his bottle of Red Stripe to his mouth staring deep into Chandelle's eyes.

Oh, this brotha got some game. I'm curious to see where this is going so I guess I'll play along for awhile. It's still too early to go lay down without getting up in the middle of the night even though I'm wore the hell out.

"Oh I'm sure you're used to a compliment or two." Chandelle said throwing the ball back into his court.

"My name is Xavier Barnes. And yours?"

"Chandelle Carter. Nice to meet you.

"What brings you to St. Croix Ms. Chandelle?"

"Chandelle is fine. I'm in the process of moving here. Like I mentioned earlier, I just flew in today. I'm meeting my real estate agent tomorrow after I handle some other business."

"Really? St. Croix is blessed to have you here. We'll have to exchange phone numbers." Chandelle's eyebrows rose hearing his last comment thinking he might be moving a little fast in making the assumption that she was interested.

"I see you're taken aback a bit by my comment. I was just stating the exchange in case you don't have any luck with your agent. I have a wonderful contact here who I'm sure can get you into something nice and quickly without all the hassles."

"I didn't mean to come across as rude. I'm sure your intentions are honorable."

"No offense taken." The bartender served Chandelle her drink and placed it on a napkin in front of her. Recovering from her embarrassment she continued,

"So Xavier, you don't mind my calling you Xavier do you?"

"Please do. I'd love to think I've met a friend."

Smiling Chandelle continued, "What do you do for a living on this beautiful island?"

"I'm an investment banker, stocks, bonds that sort of thing."

"That sounds exciting. You're probably never bored at your job. Never know what you're going to get any given day." Xavier chuckled at her response.

"That's a good way of putting it. It can be stressful at times handling investments for others. You know how people are about their money."

"I can imagine. Sounds too risky for me. I just probably don't know enough about it." Chandelle was anticipating he would talk more about what he does in hopes she get some insight on how she could grow the nest egg she had put away.

"May I ask what your plans are?" Disappointed he didn't give away secrets she answered.

"I'm looking for a couple of investments myself. I was thinking about opening a business once I conduct some research."

"Well, I'm impressed." Xavier excused himself taking a call.

Okay, this man is going to get my phone number. He definitely gets brownie points for seeming to be interested in me rather than himself. Any chance a brotha gets to brag on shit he thinks might impress a sista, you can't get him to shut the fuck up. Unless, he's sheisty and straight up lying about what he does for a livin'. Either way I'm about to find out.

"Chandelle, I'm going to have to call it an evening. That was a very important call and I must leave. It has been a pleasure. Please take my card. It has my personal cell phone and office number. Please call me tomorrow. I'd like to continue our conversation maybe over dinner?" Chandelle looked at his business card and placed it in her purse. Chandelle smiled knowing she was going to take him up on his offer. She wanted to make friends who could at least help her get acquainted with the island.

"I'll call you some time in the afternoon. I should be done with my business at around two or three then I've got to shop for a few things and hopefully I'll be done in time for dinner."

Xavier took Chandelle's hand and gently placed a kiss.

"I'll be waiting to hear from you." Xavier paid the bill and Chandelle watched him walk towards the beach- front shops to the parking lot at the rear.

Chapter 2

Rena stared at the phone on the side table contemplating whether to call Chandelle or not.

That girl has been gone for over twelve hours. She could've at least called a sista and let her know she arrived safely. Pacing back and forth across the living room floor Rena picked up the phone placing it back down on its base.

I need to come clean and tell her the truth that I didn't lose my passport. I'm just gonna get that money from our package to prevent her from coming back to the states and possibly face charges. Besides, she didn' kill Ricky, I did. She took enough risks already ensuring me and the girls would be financially straight for a long time.

It'd been three days since Rena confronted Ricky about paying what he lost on the streets. Rena drove to their apartment and waited in the bedroom for Ricky to get home. Hearing a car door close, Rena looked out the bedroom window and saw his car parked across the street. She listened for him to enter the apartment and close the door behind him. Ricky ran up the steps, walked into the bedroom and pushed the bed towards the wall giving him access to the hardwood floor decorated with a brown oriental throw rug. Rena watched as he removed his arms from his backpack and his gun from his waistband and placed them on the bed. Ricky kneeled to the floor pulling back the rug then loosened the floorboards underneath. Silently, Rena moved from behind the door and approached Ricky from behind.

"What the fuck are you doing ?" Rena moved closer to Ricky to get a better look at what was hidden in the floor. *"I saw you at the casino earlier. You were supposed to follow the plan and meet me at the house so I could pay you what I promised!"* Startled, Ricky grabbed his stash and stood pushing Rena backwards so he could place the money and brick in his backpack.

"What the fuck do it look like? You talk too damn much. You shoulda just got your loot then paid me my money and kept steppin'. When you told me you were planning on robbing a casino, I figured why just take your shit when I can get paid from all you bitches?" Rena dashed for the gun sliding back the chamber.

"Dirty motha fucka!" Rena pulled the trigger shooting Ricky twice in the chest.

****

Rrring!

Chandelle rolled over in the dark reaching for her cell phone. Realizing the time she panicked when she noticed it was four o'clock in the morning. She hardly had a moment to say hello before she heard Rena on the line.

"What's up girl? Why couldn't you call me and let me know that you made it okay? You know I was worried about you?"

"Damn! You scared me to death calling me this late!" Chandelle yawned before sitting straight up in the bed and plumping the pillows behind the small of her back to get more comfortable.

"I'm sorry I didn't call. I got off the plane and made it to the hotel and was so excited I ran down to the beach. Rena it is beautiful. I can't wait till you get here. Anyway, when you didn't hear anything you should've known everything was cool."

"*Whatever*. The police were here again today. They came by to question me again about Ricky's death and asked if I was able to remember anything that may help them out in their investigation."

"Damn. What did you tell them?"

"I didn't tell them shit. I let 'em know that I didn't know anything. All I told them that I would be looking for a new place because I didn't feel safe staying here anymore. You know I laid it on pretty thick but that one cop that was here kept giving me these strange looks as if I was lying or he was waiting for me to slip up with my story."

"You're doing the right thing Rena. Keep it short and sweet. As long as you don't have anything to tell you won't have to worry about slipping up on a lie."

"True. It's crazy though. It's as if he can see right through me or something. I gotta get outta here."

"Did they say if they were looking at anybody for possible leads?"

"They didn't say. They just said that they believe it was drug related. You know, drug deal gone bad."

"Well that's good. How long do you think it's going to take before your passport arrives? If you move before it comes in the mail you should call and make arrangements to pick it up. You don't want to fool around and worry about having different addresses on your identification and it causing you problems with getting here." Rena began pacing the floor listening closely to what Chandelle was telling her not thinking about the possibility of her id becoming a problem. She contemplated telling Chandelle the truth that her passport wasn't lost at all but the truth about why she'd stayed in the states.

"I didn't even think about that. I'm not even gonna worry about it. When I plan to leave here I'll be on a plane to the islands girl. That was just some bullshit. Anyway, are things coming together as planned?"

"Yeah. So far, so good, for the first day. I'm going to the bank first thing in the morning then I'm meeting with the realtor. I should have a place for us by the end of the week or early next week. I got to get some shopping in. believe it or not I don't have shit to wear so I'm going to get my shopping on tomorrow too. But *girl* let me tell you. I went for a night cap earlier and met this fine ass man. Girl, he looks like Idris Elba with locks."

"What? I got the business meetings part but I know you ain't down there getting your groove on already. Especially since you just broke things off with Derrick. You need to handle your business first then you can play later."

"Look who's trying to give relationship advice. I got this. I'm just looking and admiring. But he did give me some ideas."

"What kind of ideas?" Rena walked towards her kitchen opening the refrigerator for a bottle of water.

"Well he's an investment banker and makes investments for his clients. He's also into buying and selling stocks and bonds."

"And what does that have to do with you?" Rena said removing the cap and swallowing a sip of water.

"Well, I was thinking that we have a couple of dollars in the bank that we can live off of comfortably for some time but we'd have to be careful with our spending and you have responsibilities that we have to take care of there. Even with the money from the casino we won't be living large like I'd like to. Don't get me wrong I'm not trying to be greedy or do nothin' illegal."

"Too late for that don't you think?" Rena said laughing.

"We should start thinking about investing our money and make it grow so we don't have to worry about being broke and ever having to worry about working again. I'm not trying to work unless I'm working for myself."

"I feel you. I know about the debt here Chandelle. I also know that it's my responsibility and not yours to worry about my mothers' medical expenses. I don't expect the bills to come out of your share." Rena thought about her mother who was being given dialysis treatments three times a week without medical insurance. She recently paid a bill to the hospital for twenty-thousand dollars for just three months of treatments.

"You now we have that package that can take care of most of that."

"I thought we agreed that the package would stay put until we need it. Try to pretend it doesn't exist. Besides, it's too hot right now to mess with that."

"I know. I know. Listen, it's late sweetie. I'll call you in a day or two to check in. Go back to sleep. I'm glad everything is okay with you. I'm fine and if you need to know anything before I get back in touch I'll call you."

"Okay. Love ya."

"Love you too. Bye."

Chapter 3

Xavier made the twenty- minute trip from Rodney Bay to Gros Islet for a meeting to see his old roommate and friend Brian Carver who owned a restaurant by Reduit Beach. Xavier and Brian met while attending Howard University some twelve years earlier and have been close friends ever since. Xavier had been a political science major where his goal was to become a lawyer and return home to the islands to open a law practice. He was introduced to brokering and the stock market by one of his professors. The students in Mr. Gleasons class were encouraged to make a small investment using an online broker then report on their investment choices. Xavier fell in love with the whole idea of buying and selling commodities and did very well with his portfolio and was able to make a sizable profit from his trading. He later introduced his fraternity brothers to the market and charged a small fee to handle their portfolios. Brian on the other hand, came from a fairly wealthy family and received a monthly allowance that he chose to invest in future trading that involved a high risk investment with a potential for strong initial returns but could also result in significant losses as well. By the time both men reached graduation both had portfolios in excess of a million dollars. Brian loved women and soon found himself involved in a scandal at the school where he was accused of raping an undergrad student. His parents who were shocked when they heard, hired the best lawyers and not long after acquitted of all charges. Brian was in his sophomore year when his parents then all but disowned him stating that he'd embarrassed the family and would not be able to return to New York and work for the family business. Xavier remembered their conversation as if it were yesterday.

"Brian man, I know you're in a fucked up situation right now but I may be able to help you out. Why don't you come back home with me and get a fresh start? Don't look at it as the end of everything but as the beginning you've always wanted."

"What the hell am I gonna do in the islands man? I can see going down there and layin back for a while and chill but then what am I supposed to do?"

"You have over a mil in your portfolio. Why not let me manage your funds as I have been doing and think about opening your own business. You've always talked about owning your own restaurant. I'll even look out for you man and take it easy on you with the fees." Xavier laughed aloud.

"What's so funny man?"

"Nothin man, seriously though, I was thinking that you'd actually be helping a brotha out. I'm trying to get this brokerage business off the ground and I'd already have a testimony from a satisfied customer on my resume. I really wasn't sure if I was going to try to join a firm or go home and do my own thing."

Xavier continued to convince Brian describing the beautiful women and business possibilities in St. Croix. Brian didn't take much and moved a month after graduation, buying a condo in Rodney Bay overlooking the beach and a restaurant he called *The Island Room* in Gros Islet.

Xavier pulled his candy apple red Porsche 911 into an open space in front of the restaurant and set the alarm before entering the restaurant. As usual, the swanky stucco style restaurant was packed with the mid- day patrons and waitresses carrying orders from the kitchen for the lunch crowd. The restaurant was large in comparison to the other businesses on the street. Gros Islet once a very small village that was later upgraded into a town thanks to its growing population and tourism. The *Island Room* had twenty tables and floor to ceiling windows throughout. It was tastefully decorated with an island motif of white table cloths covering each table, candlelabras in each corner of the room and a four tiered candelabra hung in the middle of the room giving the dining room an heir of elegance. Gardenia arrangements were placed on each table along with palm trees tastefully positioned near the entryway. A wet bar was centered to the back of the restaurant entertaining a small crowd while Gregory Isaac could be heard softly in the background. Xavier spoke to a few of the bus boys as he made his way to the back office to meet with Brian.

Damn how I hated this day to come but Brian has to understand the risk in playing the market. How will I make him understand that he lost a third of his investment? He trusted mw to do the right thing. He asked me not to buy that damn stock and I went behind his back and did it anyway hoping he and I would walk away with a cool five if the stock had just stayed its course. Brian opened the door as Xavier approached to knock.

"What's up Xavier? You called me for this meeting and you're late. What is so important that it couldn't wait until tomorrow?" Brian opened the door allowing Xavier entry into the spacious office offering him a seat in the leather lounge chair off to the right of his mahogany desk. Xavier noticed that Brian was already dressed for the dinner crowd. Brian stood six feet and ladies labeled him boyishly handsome. His brown skin donned a tapered bald fade while his medium build wore the latest Armani suit from the spring collection. He swore he resembled Taye Diggs but taller and he's seen at the restaurant with a different woman every night of the week when he felt like being bothered. Brian took pride in greeting his customers in the restaurant and made sure they enjoyed their meal or it was on the house.

"You want a drink? I have some of that Dewars on the bar you like."

"No. I'm cool. I'm supposed to meet with this honey in a couple of hours for drinks and dinner."

"That's what's up. Well relax and tell me what I can do for you."

"Man I wish I was here to give you some good news." Brian walked towards the bar and fixed himself a drink then turned to give Xavier his full attention.

"I messed up man. I messed up real bad." Brian took a seat at the stool near the bar.

"Messed up how? Come on man give it to me straight."

"Remember when I told you about that investment last week that was going to set us up for life?

"Yeah, I remember. What about it?" Brian said getting up from the stool approaching Xavier.

"Back up and sit down man. Just listen to what I have to say". Xavier rose from his chair and walked towards the bar reaching for a glass to mix a drink. Adding ice and two fingers of Dewars, Xavier brought the drink slowly to his lips tossing it back taking it to the head. Using his shirt sleeve to wipe his mouth he paused briefly starring at his long-time friend,

"Despite your apprehension, I went ahead and made that call to Charles and bought a thousand shares of that stock for the new internet software company. I know you didn't want any parts of it but Charles assured me it was a winner and I took his word for it. I believed him man. Look how much money we've made on his tips. The stock started out well in the beginning of the week but took a nose dive over the last couple of days." Brian remained silent which seemed like forever. Five minutes had passed and Brian never moved a muscle or muttered a word. *Damn! Brian is awfully calm. Please don't let him try to kill me up in here. I'd hate for it to get physical in here.*

Gritting his teeth Brian began to speak slowly enunciating every syllable in his word.

"How- much- of- my- money- did- you- lose?" Brian walked towards Xavier stopping short of the bar to wait for an answer.

"A half mil man." Angrily Brian swiped clean the top of the bar sending liquor bottles, glasses and a tub of ice to the floor. Brian was aware that the market was a gamble but he also knew that he wouldn't be in this position if Xavier had listened. Xavier moved swiftly behind the bar holding his arms out giving space between him and Brian.

"Hold up man! Listen! Let me talk to you! I can fix this!" Xavier yelled walking backwards rounding the end of the bar.

"Your money wasn't the only money I lost! I lost some of mine too!"

"I don't give a fuck about how much of your money you lost! I'm ready to kill your fucking ass!"

"Brian I can fix this! I can get all your money back plus hook you up with a little something extra. All I have to do…" A hard knock was heard at the door interrupting Xavier in mid-sentence. The door opened and one of the waiters from the restaurant peeked his head in. Looking around the room the waiter said,

"Brian is everything okay? I heard all the noise so I figured I'd come and take a look."

"Yes, Jason everything is fine. Thanks for checking. We're just having a difference of opinion here. Let the staff know that I'll be out in a minute to go over the dinner menu." Jason nodded and closed the door behind him. Brian turned and looked at Xavier and straightened his tie.

"My man just saved your fucking life. But check this out. I don't give a fuck how you do it but you best get my money straight and you have till the end of the month to get it done or next time your ass won't be so lucky. Now get the hell out my office and I don't want to hear shit from you unless it's about where to pick up my ends." Brian walked out the office leaving Xavier thinking about what to do next.

****

Xavier drove along the highway paralleling the shoreline going through his mental black book of clients he could call for a quickie investment deal. The phone rang interrupting his thoughts.

"Hello."

"Hey Mr. Xavier, I was giving you a call to find out if I can still take you up on the offer for dinner. Are you still up for a bite to eat and maybe a couple of drinks?"

"Hi, Chandelle. Um, you caught me at a bad time. I just left my business meeting and I'm riding down the coast heading back home now." Xavier forgot about having a late lunch with Chandelle and after the days meeting wasn't sure if he was up for company.

"Oh, I'm sorry. I thought you would be down by now. I will give you a chance to get settled in and I can call you later for dinner. In fact we can cancel for another time. You don't sound like you're up for company. Well, perhaps a rain- check then. I hope you feel better"

"Yeah that may be a good idea. My meeting didn't go very well and I do have some work to do for one of my clients."

"Oh, Okay well I'll take a rain check. Call me when you get a chance."

"Hey baby, hold up, wait a minute. I think that dinner with a beautiful lady is definitely in order for tonight." Xavier said revisiting the last conversation he had with Chandelle and believed that maybe she could be the answer to his problem with Brian.

"Are you sure? You sound a little hesitant and I know that you're busy. I fully understand if you have to cancel."

"Not at all. I'm sure you're just what the doctor ordered to brighten a hectic day. Let's make plans for a late dinner. Let's say I come by your hotel and pick you up around seven. Is that okay with you?"

"Yes, I'll be ready."

"I'll see you then."

Xavier pulled into the cul-de-sac leading to his condo and dialed the *Breakstone Steakhouse* to make dinner reservations for the evening.

Chapter 4

Rena walked down the hallway of Allegheny General Hospital to room 412 after receiving a call that her mother had to be taken by ambulance after passing out. Rena tapped slightly on the door and entered only to find her mother sleeping soundly and hooked up to an IV in her left arm. Sitting in a chair on her right was her Aunt Cara and her cousin Misha who was sitting close beside her.

"Hi Aunt Clara. Misha. How's mommy?"

"The doctor just left. He said her sugar was low but she should be fine. He wanted to keep her overnight for observations but she should be okay to leave in the morning. Since you're here, I'll let you have my seat and you and Misha can talk while I go get some coffee. I'll be back in a little while. You want anything?"

"No auntie I'm fine. Thanks." Rena walked towards her aunt and hugged her as she got up to leave the room.

"Hey, Misha what's good with you? I appreciate your calling me and waiting here with mommy till I got here."

"Girl, you know you don't have to thank me. I love my auntie. You know I wouldn't let anything happen to her. Besides, I had to bring my mother over here anyway cause the ambulance driver wouldn't let her ride with your mother. She was acting all hysterical and everything. They didn't want her upsetting her making the situation any worse than it already was. But I do want to talk to you about something."

"What's that?" Rena asked suspiciously after Mishas voice lowered to where it was hardly audible.

"My brother and his mouth are at it again. You know he is the ear on the streets. He gave you the heads up bout Ricky and he said that there are some brothers on the streets asking some serious questions bout how he died and what happened to his stash."

"Yeah, Nico told me about what was going on with Ricky in the streets. But I don't know what to say about his death or stash. Why are you bringing this up to me anyway? I'm trying to let all that shit be in my past where it belongs. I just want to get on with my life."

"He said that the dude he owes money to want to talk to you cause you were the last person to see him alive and they think you might know something."

"I can't help them. I will tell them the same thing that I told the police. The police confiscated his money and I don't know anything 'bout no stash." Rena lowered her voice after seeing her mother stir in her sleep hoping she didn't overhear their conversation.

"Just watch your back girl. I thought all that shit was over too. For some reason, they ain't letting it go and I don't want to see you get hurt because they think you're holding out or lying to them."

"I'll be careful but I really don't want to talk about this anymore. I don't want mommy to hear or worry. All I'm worried about right now is her getting better. She doesn't need any setbacks or to be worried about me. I'm supposed to be moving soon but can't until I know she's stable."

"That's another thing, Chandelle got out of town awfully quick. What's up with that?"

"What do you think? She recently was let go at her job and she was a suspect in Ricky's killing. Not only that, she was brought into the precinct behind that crazy ass Angela and she got killed so can you blame her?"

"I guess not. It's just that Chandelle has always been so correct. The goody-goody kind. I would've thought she woulda tried to clear her good name before leaving town. That's all I'm saying."

"Everybody gets tired Misha. Chandelle and Derek broke up and she didn't feel as if she had any- one or anything left. She knew she had me but I was the one dating Ricky. It was all just a bit too much. She didn't want to drag me under. She knew I knew that he was a drug dealer and all that would've come out in court. It's just too sticky. I would've left too."

"Yeah, we would've left but it's just not like her. She…"

"Let it go Misha!" Rena said frustrated that Misha wouldn't let it go. Rena got up from the chair leaning over her mother to pull the blankets up to her chin.

"I have to go. Let me go find my mother. I need to pick my son up from his fathers in an hour. Are you going to be okay?"

"Yeah, I'll be fine. Look Misha, I appreciate your letting me know what's up. I know your heart is in the right place and you're trying to look out but I just got to find a way to take care of mommy and get out of here to start all over again. I'm even trying to send for her once I get myself settled."

"Alright, cool. Call me if you need me." Misha gave Rena a hug grabbed her purse and headed for the door.

I'm so sick of this shit I don't know what to do! I shouldn't have sent all my money to Chandelle. I barely have money for living expenses and surely can't pay mommy's bills on what I have. I can't ask Chandelle for money cause she'll get suspicious about my going to the islands and I can't take the drugs with me. I got to get rid of this shit without raising any suspicions in the streets and get this money.

"Rena? Is that you? Are you okay baby?"

"Of course mommy." Rena placed a warm smile on her face not recognizing that her mother awakened and was watching her.

"How are you feeling mommy? I was told that your sugar was low and you passed out."

"I took my insulin this morning but I guess that I didn't have enough to eat this morning. I've been running around with your aunt and just felt dizzy and passed out. I just have to be more careful is all."

"Mommy you have got to be more careful. You now diabetes is nothing to play with. The doctor said…"

"I know what the doctor said." Ms. Chalmers stated cutting her off abruptly.

"What is going on with you? I may not have been myself lately but I'm not stupid Rena. The streets weren't just paved when you were born. I've been hearing some disturbing things and your name has been mixed up in it. Now tell me what's going on."

Shocked Rena leaned back wondering what exactly her mother had heard and how much or what she should tell her.

"Don't look so surprised young lady. I raised you. I know when something is going on. I didn't pay it much mind at first but then when you stopped calling and stopped coming by I started to figure there must be some truth in it. You aint mixed up with them drugs is you? I heard something 'bout you being mixed up with drugs. It was that no good Ricky wasn't it? I knew he was no good from the first day you brought him by the house.

"No mommy. You know better than that." Rena answered.

"My friend Bonnie who lives in the same building complex as Chandelle told me that Chandelle got herself mixed up in some trouble and the police were by there asking her some questions. She also said that you were staying with her and all of a sudden rumor had it that Chandelle came into a lot of money and moved. Now you tell me what part of that is true and don't try to lie to me cause I haven't heard a thing from Chandelle and she calls me on the daily. I also know she ain't working that job of hers no more either."

Rena was surprised at how much her mother knew even though she was missing a lot of the key information of the story. She could never tell her mother that she and Chandelle robbed a casino. She also didn't want to tell all of Chandelle's business about her ex boyfriend Derek and his being married to crazy ass Angela who died during the casino heist. Least of all she didn't want to tie in Ricky's death to her and Chandelle even though she knew Ricky was killed with his death being linked to a drug deal gone bad. She couldn't keep Ricky's information from her because it made all the papers and the evening news.

"Mom it's nothing to worry about. I did stay at Chandelle's for a couple of days because Ricky and I were fighting. She was good enough to let me stay there until we tried to work things out." Exhaling loudly she continued, "Chandelle got fired from her job. She was too embarrassed to say anything to anybody about it. She'd been warned about being late and when she punched in after her start time, she was let go. That is why you haven't heard anything from her. She's trying to get herself together before she can face anybody. She moved because she couldn't afford the place where she was staying. I offered for her to move in with me but after what happened to Ricky it didn't work out. I decided as you know, that I couldn't stay there anymore with all that happened and she needed something right away. I'm going to call her later and let her know that you are worried about her and she should give you a call."

"MmmHmm. I'm sure there is more to the story than what you're telling me. I raised both of you to be more responsible than you are and I can't understand how you two get this old and start acting stupid. What did the police go by there for?" Ms. Chalmers asked, propping herself up on a pillow.

"Dag mom! You got me telling you all her business. She should be telling you not me. She was in an incident on the highway with this woman named Angela. Angela was Derek's ex and she was crazy as hell. Angela tried to run Chandelle off the road. Remember that incident on the news last week you heard about? That was Chandelle." Rena rose from her chair helping her mother with her pillow hoping her mother was satisfied with the answers she gave in an effort to cure her curiosity.

"A whole lot of stuff has happened to that child in the last week or so hasn't it? Poor thing. I know she is about to lose her mind. What are the police saying about that woman chasing her on the road like she done lost her mind? I hope they lock her behind parts up. Was she drunk or something? What's wrong with people these days?"

"Something like that mom. The police got to the bottom of it. Chandelle's okay and the police seem to be satisfied."

"Mommy you need to rest. The doctor told auntie that you should be leaving here in the morning. I'll stay till you fall asleep then I'll be here to get you in the morning."

"Don't try to change the subject Rena. I still don't think you're telling me everything. You're acting too fidgety. But I'm going to tell you this then I'm going to let it go cause you're grown and you're going to do what you want to do anyway just like you did with that boy Ricky. I told you he wasn't no good." She said rolling her eyes. Ms. Chalmers grabbed Renas hand in hers and continued, "I hope you and Chandelle know what you're doing. I can't get in them streets like I used to do when the two of you were younger and would get in trouble. I also know that stuff happens and we all make mistakes. But you better think about the repercussions of whatever the two of you are thinking before you do it. It's rough out here these days. Folks don't play by the same set of rules like they used to. You can fool around and get yourselves killed. I know you have been taking care of me and now that you lost your job times are tough. But don't worry yourself about me. I applied for assistance to help me with my bills and when the good Lord is ready to take me he's going to take me."

"Mommy please don't talk like that!"

"Hush girl! I'm just letting you know that I'll be okay. I have some money put up. It's not a lot but it's enough to take care of me for awhile. So don't do anything stupid thinking you have to take care of me. I don't want that on my conscious so this needed said. I love you and pray for you everyday hoping you get what the Lord has planned out for you."

"I love you too mommy. I'm fine and believe me, Chandelle's fine too. You know I'm hoping to leave town soon to get a fresh start and I have plans on bringing you with me."

"I don't know if I want to go with you chile. The family is here and I'm too old to be traipsing around with you and Chandelle. You two will kill me before this here diabetes will, trying to keep up with y'all. Now I had my say so I'm going to get me some rest. You go on and go. It's already dark out and I don't like you driving in the dark. I'll have the nurse call you in the morning when I'm ready to go."

"Okay mommy. Sleep well. I'll see you in the morning."

Damn that Ms. Bonnie! I forgot her old ass lived in Chandelle's building. She needs to mind her own damn business. I gotta make sure I get in touch with Chandelle and have her call mommy so she won't worry herself to death. The last thing I need is to have her mixed up in this shit because she's worried asking my cousins questions. I really don't need this shit right now.

Rena walked down the hallway stopping at the nurses' station to leave her information for updates on her mother. She also asked that they contact her in the morning and let her know what time her mother would be released. Heading down the hallway she stopped at the elevator anxious to get to the garage and get home. Rena anxiously hurried home. Starting the car she was blinded by the headlights of a black SUV behind her. She flipped her rearview mirror up to deflect the light then proceeded out the garage making a right on North Avenue heading home. Ten minutes later Rena was pulling into her apartment complex. Rena parked the car and got out. She was again blinded by the same headlights of the black SUV she seen at the hospital. The truck pulled inches from her. Frozen and shook, she knew it was foolish to run because whoever it was behind the tinted windows of the monstrosity was going to catch up with her sooner or later. She tried to remain calm knowing that if they wanted to rob and kill her they'd leave no witnesses to tell about it. It was too risky out in the open of an apartment complex because anyone looking out their window could ID them. If they wanted her dead they had the opportunity to do so in the darkness of the hospital garage.

What the fuck? I can't run. Please Lord don't let me die like this. Damn! All I wanted to do was go in the house, fix myself a drink and make a couple of phone calls.

Suddenly, the lights went out and the driver side and front passenger doors opened. Two men exited wearing black leather jackets with matching black skullies, jeans and sneakers. Both stood about six feet tall but it was the driver that approached Rena and spoke first.

"Whassup baby? Damn! Ricky did say his bitch was fine as hell!" He said eyeing her up and down then looking back at his friend who had an evil grin on his face.

"Do I know you?" She said trying to hide her fear and holding her composure.

"Naw baby, but we can get to know each other." He said chuckling reaching to touch the side of her cheek.

Slapping his hand away from her face Rena said, "I don't think so. What do you want?"

"I think you know what I want. Ricky made me a lot of money. But the nigga still owes."

"What's that got to do with me? I don't sell no drugs and I don't know nothing about what you talkin about or he owed or who he sold to."

"Maybe not. But word is you and Trey were the last to see him alive. Trey is dead so that leaves you to tell me where my package is. I want my shit."

"Again, I don't know nothing 'bout your *shit.*" Rena felt the burning of the back- hand that landed across her left cheek. Soothing her face she stepped back to try to get around the towering man in front of her. Grabbing her by the neck he allowed just enough air to breathe. He whispered in her ear,

"You have a week to find my package. I'll be back. If you don't have my ends you're a dead bitch. You feel me?"

Rena nodded yes as he slammed her against the car. Gasping for air, Rena braced herself against the car and tried to gather her wits. She watched as they drove away. Slowly, Rena headed towards her apartment.

Chapter 5

"Hey girl, I didn't expect to hear from you so soon. I was just on my way out." Chandelle listened as Rena cried. "Rena? What's wrong? Are you crying?"

"Chandelle. I...We... Got a problem." Rena broke down crying louder into the phone.

"Get it together Rena! What's wrong?"

"I just got back from seeing my mom in the hospital and I was followed home by these guys who were friends of Ricky's."

"What? Hold up! Slow down Rena. First tell me why mommy is in the hospital and what friends of Ricky's followed you home?"

"Mommy'll be okay. She was out earlier with Aunt Clara at the mall all day. Her sugar was low and she passed out and they took her to Allegheny General .She'll be fine. She's coming home tomorrow." Rena said sniffling.

"Well, that's good. I'm glad she's alright. Now tell me what's going on with Ricky's friends."

"They followed me home from the garage at the hospital. Then they blocked me in with their truck and got out talking shit about the package."

"What about the package?"

"Dude said that Ricky worked for him and was fronted some drugs. Well, since he died before he could flip the drugs he's looking for the package. He said I was the last to see Ricky so they figure I know where the package is." Rena said crying and screaming uncontrollably.

"Pull yourself together Rena! What did you say?"

"What the fuck do you think I said? I told them I didn't know what they were talking about. He didn't believe me and said he was going to kill me and my family if I didn't give it to him. He said I have a week to get it to him."

"Fuck Rena!" Chandelle yelled across the line.

"Don't yell at me Chandelle! I wasn't the only one who wanted to keep that shit! You did too! I'm the one here being threatened. Not you! You're laying your fat ass on the beach soaking up the sun while I'm here about to die!"

"Calm the hell down Rena! You're not going to die! Just give me a minute to think. Okay, the news reported that they found fifty grand in the apartment when Ricky died and they didn't mention finding any drugs. So, his boys know the drugs are still out there somewhere. They haven't gone through your apartment yet because the police just cleaned up their investigation there this morning removing the yellow tape. But you can best believe they will find a way to get in there. So, Rena you got to get out of there tonight."

"I was going to move into a extended stay motel tomorrow anyway."

"Get out of there tonight. It's still kinda early so pack what you need and leave. If they're watching you, you'll be giving them easy access to the apartment. There's no need for you to be in the way if they decide to tear the place up. Let the landlord deal with it and he can call the police."

"Then what?" Rena asked.

"Call your cousin Nico and find out if he knows who these dudes are. Did he tell you his name?"

"No. But my cousin Misha told me earlier at the hospital that Nico told her that these brothers where asking questions… you know…concerning Ricky's death and my name came up."

"Well maybe that will work in our favor. Nico can get some useful information on these dudes and we can know who we are dealing with. Plus, he's your cousin. He doesn't want to see anything bad happen to you. I'm thinking that maybe your passport will come within the week and you can be on your way down here."

"Chandelle, I can't leave my family wide open like that! They're talking bout killing them if they don't get their shit!"

"Okay, I hear you. What if Nico finds out who they are and you send them a message? I'm thinking that if we explain to them that we don't know anything but we're willing to give them some money for their troubles, this shit will go away."

"Hmmm, That might work. But that'll mean we're gonna have to find jobs. That was the purpose of us getting that money in the first place. So we could retire and take care of ourselves and our families."

"Rena, you won't have to worry about a job if your ass is dead! Besides, I told you I'm working on something on this end. I'm meeting this guy tonight. He may be the answer to our problem. Thank goodness we moved the package out of there. If they're following you they won't find anything. Just lay low. We've got it in a safe place where nobody's going to find it."

"We shoulda put it in a locker somewhere so if I needed to leave town in a hurry I could snatch it up and roll." Rena said as matter of fact.

"You're joking right Rena? This ain't no damn movie! Only stupid asses hide drugs in a train station or bus depot . In fact those ass holes are probably thinking you did something like that so they can catch you picking it up then kill your dumb ass! Just leave it alone til' we need it and it's safe."

"Alright. So if your plan works out and I get there in a week or two, we'll have some money to live on? You know I still have obligations here."

"I don't know but I'm gonna find out. We might have to work for a while. I don't know how fast the return is on market investments. But if the returns are what I think they are, we won't have to work another day in our lives." Chandelle listened as she heard Rena sigh with relief. She continued, "Just keep in touch and let me know where you're staying and what the word is on the streets. Listen, I hate to let you go but I gotta meet Xavier in about twenty minutes. That's the brotha I was telling you about. Take care and don't forget to call me. Tell your mother I'll call her tomorrow. Bye."

"Bye Chandelle."

Damn! I don't want to work! I risked my ass robbing a casino and killing that asshole of a man I was dealing with. I took his shit too so I wouldn't never have to work again. I'm gonna' follow the plan but if I can get those drugs flipped, I'm damn sure going to do it.

****

Xavier held the small of Chandelle's back as they waited to be seated by the maitre d of the restaurant.

"Did I tell you how absolutely gorgeous you look tonight? Red is definitely your color." He said whispering in her ear so that only she could hear.

It's a damn shame I'm gonna have to take her for all her money. She's fine as hell. She might even have what it takes to be Mrs. Barnes. Maybe I can show her a legit investment gain and make things up to her later.

Chandelle didn't turn around in fear of telling on herself showing the redness of the blush she was wearing on her cheeks.

"Again you flatter me Mr. Barnes."

"Not flattery Chandelle. I call it as I see it. I hope we won't be this formal all evening. I'd really like to get to know you." The maitre d showed them to their table handing them each a menu.

"Everything sounds delicious. I don't know what to order."

"Well, allow me to order for you. They are known for their lobster. How does that sound to you?"

"That'll be fine. I haven't had a good lobster in a long time." The waiter approached offering a hearty red wine and delivered their order to the chef.

"Now that we have that out the way, we can continue our conversation where we left off. How did your meeting go with the realtor? Did you find something that you like?"

"She showed me a couple of nice places but not exactly what I'm looking for. My plans have just recently changed and I don't think that I want something as permanent as I had planned. My best friend who is like a sister to me will be living with me and we decided to downsize our plans. We're thinking that we'll find something a littlemore permanent when she gets here so she can have some input on the place as well as on location." Xavier's eyebrows rose in concern after hearing they need to downsize their plans.

"Is that all? I mean is it only that she wishes to have input in the location?" Xavier lowered his gaze trying to be coy in asking about her finances. "I hope I'm not overstepping my boundaries. It's just that as I mentioned before, I have a great realtor that may be able to help you and if I had an idea of what you're looking for I could give her your information and have her meet you at your convenience."

"I wasn't offended at all. She has a say in our investments. I may have to send her some money because she'll be in the states a little longer than planned. So, I just want to get a small two bedroom and scout out a place where we can start a business."

"What kind of business?" Xavier asked moving forward.

"Well, I worked for an accounting firm in Pittsburgh. I assisted with teaching the firms new clients how to use their software. I also dabbled in writing programs and fixing glitches when they arose. So, I'm thinking we can offer similar services here for the local businesses."

"Beautiful and smart. Now I'm thinking how your services could work for me and my small business."

"Oh. Now I'm impressed. I thought you worked for some bank or company that deals in investments."

"I do. But I also work for myself for special accounts, mostly friends and close acquaintances. I do it for them so they don't have to pay all the fees they'd normally have to by being a client of Morton and Meyers."

"That's generous of you Xavier." She chuckled,

"I'm getting paid for my services Chandelle. A brotha got to make money too. I don't want you thinking that I'm doing it for free. I'm not robbing anybody but we're all paid." Chandelle smiled and wondered if his generosity would include her if she wanted in on his investment expertise.

If I can get him to take me on as a client, sending Rena money may not hurt as much as I thought it would. It would leave more money to invest and we can receive more on the back end. Interrupting her thoughts the waiter placed their orders on the table and asked if there was anything else they needed.

"No, that's all for now, thank you." Xavier answered. Chandelle sliced into her lobster savoring its flavor.

"You're right Xavier this lobster is delicious." Wiping her lips she swallowed and continued,

"Xavier, how do you know what to invest in and what's going to make money for your clients?"

"Well, clients usually like to get involved with what is new on the market. If for example a pharmaceutical company comes out with a new drug, clients want to invest to get in on the ground floor. If it's a success there would be a lot of money to be made. But some investors invest for the long haul and like the safer commodities. You know companies that have been around for a long time. Companies like General Electric, Shell gasoline, Heinz etc. Even some of the newer companies like Yahoo and Google are pretty safe because they have proven to stay around with millions of members to their credit. Companies like those are usually found in your standard 401k portfolios.

"I remember my money being invested in companies similar to those. I averaged a gain of about a thousand a year based on my investment. But you're right it is a slow process."

"Yeah, but if it doubles your money in about twenty or thirty years you're ready to retire. You can live comfortably at retirement age. You get better returns on your money than letting it sit in a savings account. Most people don't school themselves on investments and the stock market. They are at the mercy of the investment groups used by their employer. They just ask if you want low, moderate or high risk investments then they put the money where they see fit."

"I hear you. When I started working at my firm at twenty-five I asked for a high- risk investment because I knew I had forty years of employment in front of me. If I lost money I knew I would have time to get it back when the market improved."

"Smart girl. I tell clients that they should move their money only when the market overall is suffering. If the market is stable, I tell them to hold steady and move their money around, as they get closer to retiring. By forty they should start looking at safer investments until they are ready to cash out. I don't want to see my clients lose money. They lose money- I lose money. It's risky enough to invest. I can't have them not coming back. Can't have that. It's bad for business." Xavier smiled proud he added that last statement adding a touch of sincerity. *I get paid either way. Most of my high-end clients call me on the daily to move money. Most have money to burn and act as if they know more about investments than I do. They don't care about losing their cash and their arrogance brings them back every time. But she doesn't need to know that does she?*

"That makes sense. Explain the risky investments. You said they are usually new companies to the market. How do they get people to make investments?" Chandelle said finishing off her wine and placing the empty goblet on the table.

"You've finished your food. Can I order you some dessert?"

"No. I've had quite enough. Thank you."

"Then let's get out of here and we can finish up our conversation somewhere a little more comfortable. My condo isn't far from here and it has a very nice view."

"You're not trying to take advantage of me are you Mr. Barnes?"

"Not at all Miss lady. We can kick back a few drinks while I finish answering your questions. I just want to have more time to get to know who Chandelle Carter is."

"Likewise Xavier." Chandelle said with a smile on her face.

"I'd like for you to take me back to my hotel though so I can pick up my car and follow you to your condo. I'd hate for you to have to bring me back to my hotel later."

"That wouldn't be a problem. I don't mind bringing you back."

"No. I want to drive myself. It's okay, really."

"Well, let's go pretty lady."

Chapter 6

Xavier pulled the key to his apartment from his pocket opening the door to an expansive great room that led to a balcony that overlooked the beach.

"Xavier, your place is beautiful. Look at that view!" Chandelle said walking towards the balcony.

"Thanks love. Take a look around while I fix us a couple of drinks. Anything in particular?"

"Wine will be fine. Don't want anything harder, I still have to drive home tonight."

Chandelle moved from the balcony and towards the back of the condo passing the den and a guest bedroom. The final room at the end of the hall led to the master bedroom. Chandelle opened the door. Her eyes were drawn to a king sized poster bed placed in the middle of the room. The bed was donned in white sheers that canopied the top of the bed and hung over the sides to the floor on each side. In front of the bed was a wall mounted forty-six inch flat screen with a miniature bar that stood underneath. On the left was the master bath that included a spa sized tub and standing shower in white marble accented with black towels monogrammed with the letter B. Recessed lighting gave the room a soothing effect that begged you to indulge in the luxury. To the right was a balcony. Opened French doors with matching white sheers hung blowing in the slight breeze over the veranda.

"I see you found my bedroom." Xavier said holding two glasses in his hand standing directly behind Chandelle as she took in the room.

"OOH! You scared me! I didn't hear you come in." Chandelle turned facing Xavier. Xavier smiled and handed Chandelle her drink.

"I didn't mean to scare you. You want to get comfortable?"

"Not in here. I'd feel a little more comfortable in the living room. There's nowhere to sit in here anyway." Chandelle thanked him for the drink and headed back down the hallway to the living room.

I can't blame the brotha' for tryin'. If we were on better terms, I might take him up on his offer with his fine ass.

Getting situated on the couch Chandelle spoke first, "Finish telling me about the market Xavier. Besides putting your money on a risky investment for an early 401k, why would someone do that if there was a chance you'd lose your money?"

"You're all business aren't you lady?" Xavier said trying to be careful about his approach not wanting to scare her from trusting him with her money. Xavier smiled and continued,

"Many people make the investments with the new companies or products on the markets for fast returns on their money." That bit of information piqued Chandelles interest.

"They first do their homework and find out as much information they can about the investment or if they have a good broker they have it done for them then reported on the findings. That's where yours truly steps in. I'm the one who finds out all about the company and then advise on rather it's a good investment or not. If it looks profitable, the client usually invests, allow the stock to double or split then resell it in the market for a profit. Does that make sense to you?"

"Most of it does. Explain about the stock doubling or splitting." Chandelle said taking a sip of her drink eagerly waiting for his reply.

"It's like gambling. Just to make this easy to understand, lets say you buy five shares of stock at two dollars a share. That would cost you ten dollars. The next day, for any number of reasons the stock per share goes up to four dollars a share. You now made at the end of the day ten dollars so your investment is now worth twenty dollars. That is doubling your investment. Sometimes for numerous reasons the stock splits. Using the prior example, you bought for investment five shares and the stock splits. Now you have ten shares each share worth a dollar. The worth of the share goes down but you own more shares. In hope the cost per share goes up you increase your money by keeping all ten shares or you can sell five for profit keeping five of the original investment.

"Hmm interesting. When stock doubles or splits, is one better than the other?" Chandelle asked hanging on his every word.

"It depends. In the first example, you saw an immediate return on your investment earning ten dollars. The splitting stock gives you the option of owning double the shares and making more money in a long term investment . It depends again on the need of the money invested. If you need money immediately, I'd advise on investing in a hot commodity that is selling on the market. If you're investing for the future the splitting stock is worth holding on to."

"I see. Well, I'm interested in making some money from an investment but by no means am I a wealthy person trying to buy up some company in the stock market. Truthfully, I would be in and out unless there is something out there I couldn't refuse." Xavier felt he had her exactly where he wanted her. She admitted that she was interested in investing all that was left was convincing her to allow him to handle her portfolio and writing the check.

"I tell you what. Why don't you come to my office tomorrow so that I can show you up close and personal how we operate. We can then get lunch and you can meet the realtor I was telling you about."

"That sounds like a plan. I'd love to see where you work. It would be lovely if I can get out of the hotel by early next week. It's such a waste of money. It's beautiful and all but I'm ready for my own place."

"Beautiful. It's still early. I'd love to turn on some music and share some more of your company." Xavier searched through his cd collection choosing Brian Culberson's greatest hits.

"Can I have this dance?" Chandelle placed her wine on the table and folded into his waiting arms.

"I was wondering when I would have the chance to get next to you. Mmmm and you smell so deliscious." Chandelle looked into his eyes,

"Thank you." Xavier held her stare for what seemed like minutes then slowly moved his lips over hers in a passionate kiss. Moving his hand from the small of her back, he massaged her as they swayed to the sounds of the horn in the background. Suddenly, Chandelle froze in his arms breaking the passionate moment.

"Xavier, I can't do this. There's no doubt that I'm attracted to you but I hardly know you and I just got out of a relationship."

"I understand. I didn't mean to push you into anything you're not ready for. But I have to admit that I'm deeply attracted to you as well and I'm hoping we can get past any inhibitions you may have about getting to know each other better." Xavier knew he might be risking his plan but he was sincere about trying to get physical with the beautiful woman in his arms. He knew her type and the only way to get her in his bed was to convince her that he was serious about pursuing a serious relationship.

"My last relationship ended ugly. I'm in St. Croix to start a new life. There are so many things I need to do in starting over and laying roots before considering a relationship." Chandelle said turning away from his glare.

"You said you were starting over. I just hope that means you can consider allowing someone to spend time with you. There's no rush Chandelle. I'm trying to be a good friend first. Now, Come here and let me hold you. Let's continue dancing." Chandelle folded her arms around his waist and laid her head on his shoulder.

Baby you don't know how close I was to allowing you to take me to that king-size bed of yours. If nothing else I know you'd relieve some of this built up stress I have penned up inside of me. But I need you to help me make some money. I can't let some good sex get in the way. I gotta' keep my head on straight.

****

It's ten am and I already dropped mommy off at home. My lazy ass cousin is propbably still in the bed as usual. I told auntie that she needed to throw Nico's behind out her house a long time ago. Don't make no sense that his twenty-five year old behind is still living at home with his mother with no job. But at the same time, I'm glad I don't have to go out in the streets looking for him. He's about to help his cuz out of this little mess she's in. If he gets this right I'll be willing to donate to his get his shit together fund. Turning onto Curtain Street she notices the car parked in front of the house. *Good his car is parked out front.* Pulling behind his red Charger, Rena parked, exited her car and ran up the three steps leading to the house. Before she can ring the doorbell her aunt Clara opened the door.

"Hey baby, how are you? I didn't expect to see you here this morning. Did you pick up Dessa this morning?"

"Hi Aunt Clara. Yeah, she's home lying down. I'm surprised she hasn't called you yet. I stopped at the store and picked up a couple of things for her. I decided to ride by and talk to Nico for a minute. Is he up yet?"

"He's up in his room. I just took his breakfast up to him a couple of minutes ago." *Damn shame. That's why his ass won't get a job or move. She waits on him hand and foot. He'll never grow up till he can find some dummy to pick up where his momma left off.* "Don't make no sense." Rena uttered.

"Don't start Rena. It's hard to find a job these days. Plus he helps me out 'round here."

"I'm not sayin' nothing auntie."

"Nico!"

"Yeah?" Nico yelled from the upstairs bedroom.

"Rena's down here and she wants to talk to you!"

"Send her upstairs mom!" Rena headed up the stairs and knocked at the door until Nico gave her permission to enter.

"Hey baby girl, wassup wit you?"

"I'm good. I need you to do me a favor." Rena moved the three pairs of jeans Nico had strewn across the chair and tossed them to the bottom of the bed so she could sit down.

"Figured that. You never have anything to say to me unless you looking for somethin' or complainin' bout my needin' to get a job and my own spot."

"I know. Shut up Nico! You know I got much love for you." Rena smiled and blew him a kiss. "Look. I'm willing to pay for your help."

"This must be some deep shit. You ain't never come out your pockets."

"Well, I am now. Misha was at the hospital yesterday and she told me that you heard some shit on the streets about me and Ricky's drugs."

"Yeah, the boys on the block are talking. But I let 'em know that you ain't got shit and Ricky ain't never put you down with the game. I said, even if she did know somethin', what the fuck my cuz gonna do with some weight? They pretty much know you ain't even in the game like that. You ain't like these hood rats out here. Why you askin'?"

"I was approached last night Nico. These two dudes pulled up on me at the apartment threatening me about the package talkin' bout I got a week to produce it or they gonna kill me." Rena said close to tears.

"Get the fuck out of here!" Nico said jumping off the bed.

"Keep your voice down! I don't want Aunt Clara to hear us talking."

"Get the fuck outta here! What they look like Rena? What were they driving?"

"The one that was talking was about six foot tall, dark brown skin with a full beard. His friend was shorter but I didn't get a good look because the tall one was all in my face. They were driving a black Escalade."

"That sounds like Slim and Rome. Ricky used to cop from them. They're from Steubenville. Supposedly, they were frontin' Ricky enough shit to lock down the West Side. He was close to it too. Niggas from the East Side were starting to go to him to re-up. Damn girl! They ain't no joke. What you need from me?"

"Well, I was thinking. I know you're connected with a lot of friends in the streets. I was hoping that you can get a message to them for me. I'm trying to get it to them as soon as I can before the one week deadline."

"What you talkin' bout? You know something 'bout that package Rena? Them niggas on the real, ain't to be fucked wit."

"I'm not sayin that I know anything bout the drugs. But I want you to ask them if they'd be willing to take some money in exchange for them leaving me alone. I figured that they may settle for cutting their loss if they're convinced that I don't know anything about the drugs. I know they have to know about the money."

"Where you get money from Rena? You know how much drugs they talkin' bout? You got to have a lot of dough to make this go away and I ain't talking bout ten g's from a severance account from you losing your job."

"I know. But look, the police found fifty thousand on Ricky when he died and they made that public. So I'm figuring that I match that."

"First of all where the fuck you get 50 g's and word on the street is that the package was worth about two fifty." Nico said clearing space at the end of the bed to sit down.

"Two hundred and fifty thousand? I would've never thought it was worth that much!" Rena said getting out the chair and beginning to pace the floor.

" Two hundred after the package flips. Rena, you have the drugs?"

"Yeah?" Rena said giving Nico her full attention. The shocked look on his face cleared her thoughts.

"I don't mean yes. I mean… I never thought Ricky was worth that kind of money. I'm just surprised Nico that's all. Wait a minute Nico. Two hundred thousand after the package flips is different. I don't have the drugs to flip." Rena slowly sat back into the chair contemplating her next move.

"Something isn't lining up here Rena. Where you get fifty g's from? You're gonna need at least a hundred."

"It's a long story Nico. I don't want to get into right now. *Shit!* I'll get my hands on it."

"Okay, so let's say they're interested in the deal. They gonna want to know where you getting that kind of money. They gonna think you flipping that *shit* Rena."

"Convince them that it's not on the streets. They'd know if the streets were suddenly flooded with a fresh supply. Ricky hasn't been dead that long. Nobody's working Nico. I'm sure you can get word to them without facing them anyway. Pay somebody to send the message to them so you're not put in a bad situation. I don't know how the shit is done in the streets Nico! Just make it happen!" Frustrated, Rena grabbed her purse searching for her wallet. "Damn it! I don't have that much money on me. I'll cash a check at the bank to get it done."

"Rena, these dudes are gonna come lookin' for me. How soon can you have the money?"

"I can have it wired in a day."

"You know that I'm involved in this shit now don't you?"

"Baby, you were involved last night." Nico rose from the bed reaching for his jacket and keys.

"I'll let you know something by tonight. I'll pay to get the info out and you can take care of me later."

"Thanks Nico. If this works out or not, you know I'm gonna take care of you." Nico left Rena sitting in the chair watching from his bedroom window as he got in his car and drove away.

Chapter 7

Chandelle was more than a little excited about getting to the offices of Morton and Meyers brokerage firm. Xavier said that he'd meet her out front at nine sharp to give her a tour and introduce her to his friends and associates he works with. Chandelle stood calmly waiting, admiring the twenty- floor building made of convex steel and glass. She watched as the people rode the escalators through the glass.

"It's beautiful isn't it? There are only three buildings on the island that stand above ten floors. Xavier said after he creeped behind Chandelle stealing a kiss on her cheek.

"Yes, it is." Chandelle said shocked at the unexpected show of affection.

"Let's hurry in. The exchange just opened and I want you to see what we do and how busy it gets on the floor." Chandelle followed Xavier inside and waited for the elevator to climb the twenty floors before exiting to an open floor space lined with ten rows of identical cubicles.

"Wow it's so noisy. You'd think we were actually on the floor of the New York Stock Exchange." Chandelle stated looking around the room.

"Yes it is. The phones ring constantly. Our clients are watching the numbers just like we are. If they see their stock fall they call to sell or trade. We also are on the phones trying to acquire new clients." Chandelle took in the room noticing the four white walls and large Timex clocks displayed on each wall displaying the times across the globe. Slightly above it was the stock ticker tape machine recording the fluctuating shares for the day.

"I always wanted to know what the numbers on that tape meant. I would see it running under various news channels and never quite understood what they meant."

"Many people don't know what it means. It only interests those who are actively buying and trading. It's not necessary to know all the companies, just the ones where you have a current investment. Look there. See the AAPL that just came up? That stands for Apple. They are up a point so far for the day. Who knows, if you invest long enough you'll learn them all."

"I don't think so. This trading would drive me crazy. I think I'll stick with the long term portfolios and leave everything else to the experts." Chandelle winked at Xavier as he escorted her to the cubicle by the far side of the wall.

"I want you to meet a friend of mine. He's not on the phone and he's a really nice guy." Tapping him on the shoulder the gray chair swung around leaving Chandelle to look into a pair of piercing blue eyes. "Hey Mike. Meet a good friend of mine. Her name is Chandelle."

"Hi Chandelle, nice to meet you." Mike extended his hand and firmly locked on to Chandelles. "Xavier said he was bringing a friend through for a tour today. How do you like the place?"

"The building is beautiful. I'm a little overwhelmed by how busy it is here but intrigued at the same time." Chandelle said smiling.

"Well, you're in good hands. Xavier knows this place and the business inside and out. I'm sure he'll be able to answer all your questions."

"I hope so. I'm thinking of going to some investing and I'm being more and more convinced Xavier may be the man for the job." Chandelle noticed the quizzical look Mike shot at Xavier but she assured herself that she was reading something that was not there. Xavier smiled then stated he saw someone else he wanted Chandelle to meet.

"Xavier, I couldn't help but take notice of Chandelles last statement. You better not let the boss hear about you trading for your friends on the floor. His rule is that you have to turn that portfolio over to someone else. Never make it personal remember? It's bad for business if it tanks." Chandelle overheard Mike's statement and planned to revisit that bit of information later with Xavier. "Chandelle, it was very nice meeting you. Never hesitate to ask if you need anything." Chandelle was taken aback that Mike was so forward and felt there was a warning in his last statement.

"It was nice meeting you too." Chandelle waved goodbye and followed Xavier to meet another of his associates. The rest of the morning was spent moving from cubicle to cubicle while being introduced to co-workers. His mood seemed to change but he smiled when appropriate and said the correct things on cue. Chandelle figured he was growing tired of the introductions. Lunchtime soon rolled around and Xavier announced that he had reserved a table at a local eatery he frequented regularly.

"The *Blue Umbrella* is a block down the street. Let's walk and grab a couple of sandwiches and talk." After being seated, Chandelle ordered an iced tea while Xavier suggested they have the house special of the day which consisted of sandwiches and a side order of salads half off.

"Everything is always good. I think you'll enjoy your lunch."

"I'm sure I will. Xavier, do you mind if I ask you a couple of questions?"

"Sure, ask away." Xavier knew what was coming and had already decided to get her curiosity out the way early rather than wasting any time trying to reassure her later. Sure, he'd answer her questions now and hopefully not have to deal with them in the future. Besides, time was of the essence and he didn't need to procrastinate or waste any more time with her. Xavier was surprised that Mike was bold enough to comment on her intentions and he had plans on how he was going to be dealt with. He had to give it to Mike though. He knew him well and noticed the look he gave Chandelle when he laid eyes on her. Xavier recognized right away the immediate attraction.

"First, let me tell you that everyone seemed so nice. You work in a very pleasant environment even though it's so busy." Chandelle paused and took a sip of her iced tea. "But, I want to ask you something about your friend Mike." *Here it comes. I knew it.* Xavier said to himself.

"I overheard Mike say something about it being against the rules if you made some investments on my behalf. What did he mean by that?" The waitress placed the plates with sandwiches in front of them giving Xavier time to choose his next sentence carefully.

"Our boss recommends that we don't take on our friends as clients at the firm. I explained before that there is some risk in investing in the market. He advises that anyone interested and is a friend or relative, they should be referred to another broker. The commission works itself out. Any new client that someone gets goes to the individual who lost commission on the friend referral. Anyway, it's set up that way so any losses that occur are strictly business and not personal."

"I see. I appreciate your being honest with me. You know that I'm interested in building a portfolio. How were you going to handle it? Would you have told me if Mike hadn't said anything?" Chandelle asked looking him in the eyes for a- tell that he was lying.

"Of course, in fact if after today you're still interested, I was going to explain it all to you and suggest that you allow me to invest under my private practice. My intentions were to give you the chance to see that I was legit and gain some actual knowledge seeing how the brokerage firm works. I need you to feel safe with your investment. After all, you've taken a crash course. Many people spend months learning what you have in a couple of days. I think you've asked enough questions in there to write your own book." Xavier joked trying to make light of the situation.

"Well, I've decided that I'm going to do it. Just give me until tomorrow to decide whether I go with the firm or you. Okay?" Xavier was relieved that she was going to continue with the venture.

I have the rest of the day to convince you to turn your money over to me. I'll have my hands on your money by tomorrow.

"I'm glad to hear that you're willing to invest. I think it's a wise move. Making some smart investments can make you a fair amount of money." Xavier looked down at his watch checking the time.

"Chandelle, we have thirty minutes to get to the realtors office. If we leave in the next ten minutes we can make the appointment on time."

"You know, I forgot all about it. You are such a sweetheart to get that appointment for me on such a short notice. I'm finishing up here and we can leave."

I plan to be more than your sweetheart before the end of the day.

****

Eight-thirty came and went as Rena paced the floor. Every now and then she tried to concentrate on what was being shown on the television occasionally flipping to the twenty-four hour newscast hoping that a picture of Nico wasn't flashed with a caption stating he was just involved in a "accident".

I can't believe I haven't heard from Nico by now. He could've at least called me and let me know something. He knows I worry. Damn! Let me take a soak in the spa tub and try to chill. Aint nothing I can do but wait. Nico knows those streets like the back of his hand. He's fine. Rena walked to the bathroom running the water to the hottest temperature she believed she could take. After adjusting the motorized jets, she walked to the vanity and chose the almond vanilla soothing gel to pour into the water. Rena disrobed, inflated the neck pillow then climbed into the wet body massage. Leaning into the pillow and closing her eyes. She relaxed to the warm smooth sounds of Will Downing when her phone rang disrupting the soothing pellets shooting against her arm, back and legs. *Shit! Why didn't I bring that phone to the bathroom?* Rena jumped from the tub grabbing the towel that hung from the back of the door.

"Hello? Hello?" Rena waited for a response hoping that it was Nico even though she didn't recognize the number.

"Hey, Rena. You okay? You sound like you're out of breath."

"Yeah, I'm fine. I was in the spa soaking and I left the phone in the bedroom on the bed. I had to run to catch the call. Are *you* okay? I was worried to death. Why didn't you call me earlier?" Rena said with a little attitude.

"I'm cool. I got caught up but I'm calling now. Look, my man got back with me and he got the message to Slim. He said he a face-to-face. Slim wants you to bring the package and the two of you can talk."

"What the hell does that mean Nico? What is there to talk about? I was hoping that he would take the money and this whole thing would be over." Rena said shivering not knowing if what Nico said brought her a chill or the fact that she was still standing by the bed with water dripping to the floor.

"I don't know cuz. That's why I'm going with you. I wouldn't leave you out there by yourself. I told you these niggas' ain't no joke. I'm sure they gonna take the package no doubt. But I don't know what they wanna talk about. I never heard anything bout them doing something shady. They just bout their money. They'll kill a nigga bout their dough. I'm thinking that they know you was just Ricky's woman. You wasn't in the game so they should be able to be dealt with reasonably."

"I'm scared now Nico. I still don't understand what there is to talk about." Rena said rubbing her forehead.

"No matter what Rena you would have to face them in order for this to be over. Besides, a little bit of fear is always good. You will meet them expecting the unexpected. When we go in there we ain't gonna say anything more than we have to. Just keep it short and simple. Keep your mouth shut unless they ask you a question and answer those questions short and sweet. Aiight? Are you going to be able to get your hands on the money tomorrow?"

"Yeah. I'll take care of it first thing in the morning. What time and where are we supposed to meet them? I hope you suggested somewhere out in the open with a lot of traffic. I aint tryna get caught up in the hood with no hood niggas."

"It's cool. We are meeting them at one at the IHOP in Robinson. I'll come…" Rena cut in before he was able to finish his sentence.

"No. I'll come by and pick you up. I don't care whose car we drive. In fact maybe we should just take mine since they saw it the other night when they followed me back to the apartment. There's no sense in giving them too much information on how to track us down. I don't even want you to know where I'm staying just to keep you safe."

"Bet. Meet me at the crib 'round twelve. I'll talk to you later."

Rena quickly removed the towel and searched her overnight bag for a pair of shorts and a tee eager to call Chandelle and have the money wired to the bank. Rena hopped on the bed grabbing her cell phone to call Chandelle. Chandelle's hotel phone rang five times with the messaging service asking to leave a message. Hanging up, she quickly dialed her cell in hopes she answer. After three rings, Chandelle answered.

"Hey Rena. What's going on?"

"I'm so glad you answered. Girl, I was about to panic. I just got off the phone with my cousin. His boy was able to make the connect for me."

"Give me a minute to get to my hotel room. I'm just getting back from looking at condos." Chandelle took her room card from her purse and slid the card in the key lock listening for the latch to click signaling the door was unlocked.

"Okay Rena, Im in. Go ahead, what did Nico find out?"

"He told me that the brothas name is Slim. He wants to meet me tomorrow in Robinson to talk and transfer the money."

"Talk? Talk about what?" Chandelle asked.

"That's the same thing I asked. I have no idea what he wants to talk about. When Slim approached me, all he asked for was the money. Now he wants to talk. This shit got me nervous as hell. He went on to say that the package is worth two hundred and fifty g's and I need at least one hundred g's."

"Damn Rena. This might not be as easy as I thought it would be. You just can't go out there with fifty thousand dollars out in the open like that. It's too dangerous. Besides, he wants something. There's nothing to talk about."

"I know! Especially since I'm only taking fifty thousand. I'm not paying more than that Chandelle. If we pay more they will be extorting from us for life. They'd never go away. Nico said he was going with me to watch my back. His advice was to just stay cool and don't say shit unless he asks a specific question. Keep it short and simple."

"That's good advice. But you can't go in there with that money. It's not safe and you don't have anything to bargain with if you just hand it over to them. You need to have a way out. An excuse to leave or get away if you have to. Leaving the money somewhere else will give that excuse."

"Either way it's dangerous Chandelle. I'm damned if I do and damned if I don 't."

"True. But he gave you a week and you got back to him in a couple of days. He gotta figure you're on the up and up because you put this meeting together so fast. I know I wouldn't think it was a set up. I'm not saying he won't be careful but he got to think you're trying to get this over with."

"So now what? Are you going to go to the bank in the morning?"

"Yes, I'm going to the bank. I'll have the money transferred to your account. See if Nico can bring along a friend. Whatever you do, stay away from anything that would suspect them at knowing what happened to Ricky and how he died. Don't bring up the police or anything."

"So how do I explain the money Chandelle? You know they are expecting the drugs. Nico thinks something is up because I'm able to get my hands on so much cash.

"Rena! Calm down. Your cousin is the least of our problems. The worst he'll do is try to beg money from us later. Slim is our immediate concern. You know what I mean? Convince him that you don't know anything about a package but you had money put away given to you by Ricky. Better yet, tell him that there was another stash in the apartment that you knew about but the cops overlooked. There weren't any drugs and you moved out of the apartment. The bottom line is that the package is worth fifty thousand and you have fifty so he's even."

"But I wasn't honest with Nico. What do I tell him?"

"Tell him the same thing. Just tell him before the meeting. All you have to do is break Nico off a couple of dollars and he'll be straight. You know how he is."

"You're right. I'm scared shitless Chandelle."

"Scared is good. As long as you're scared you're on your toes and believable. They won't think you're trying to run a game on them. Besides, scared will keep you honest and you'll watch your back. Go to bed and get some rest. Call me after the meeting. I love you and be safe."

"*You and Nico with this scared is good shit*! I love you too. Talk to you tomorrow."

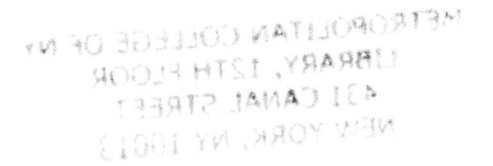

Chapter 8

Rena parked across the street from her aunts house and exited the car running to the house to ring the doorbell. Checking her watch she realized that she was cutting her twelve o'clock appointment close being as it was a little after eleven. Rena wanted to give herself time to go over the plan with her cousin and get to the restaurant before Slim. She watched enough movies to know that it would be to her advantage to pick the spot in the restaurant so she could get out safely if she needed to. Rena rang the doorbell and waited patiently for Nico to answer while wondering who else was at the house noticing two unfamiliar cars parked in front of the house.

I sure hope my aunt doesn't have a house full of her church friends here this morning. I don't have time to sit and make niceties with her today. Nico peeked out the window and opened the lock letting Rena in the house.

"What's up cuz?"

"Hey Nico. I'm glad you answered the door. I was afraid auntie would answer and had a house full." Rena said following Nico towards the steps leading to his room.

"Naw. Those cars are my boys."

"What do you mean those are your boys? We don't have time to entertain Nico. We have forty-five minutes to get to the restaurant."

"Chill Rena. I got this. After I spoke with you last night I figured we should take a couple of my boys along with us. They will take their own cars and follow us. They won't go in just sit in their cars and watch our backs. Come on up. Everything is cool." Nico grabbed Renas hand and led her to his room. Nico opened the door and she quickly noticed the room was full of smoke and two blunts were put out in the ashtray on the dresser. Two of his friends were perusing the cd collection lying beside the makeshift entertainment center made from six stacked milk crates housing a flat screen tv set on top and a stereo system underneath. The other was lounging back with his eyes closed in the chair beside the bed obviously feeling his high.

"Yo! This is my cousin Rena. This is who I was telling you 'bout." Rena nodded in acknowledgement as they gave her their full attention.

"Um Nico. Can I talk to you in private for a minute please?" Rena said turning towards Nico.

"Yeah. Can ya'll meet me out front? I need to speak to my cuz for a minute."

"It's cool." The tall heavy set guy in the chair said. "I gotta use your bathroom anyway." Rena waited for Nico's friends to leave before closing the door for privacy.

"Nico, I'm not comfortable with having your friends come along. This was supposed to be just an exchange and it would be over. Why do you think we need them along?"

"You seemed all worried last night on the phone I thought this would calm you down. Besides, it's not going to hurt to have them along. Just in case some dumb shit jumps off."

"I don't like it Nico. What did you tell them? Why do they think they're going out here besides watching my back?"

"I ain't tell 'em shit. They're my boys and I just asked them if they wanted to make a couple of dollars. They always down when it comes to makin' some paper. So they decided to make the move. I just asked them to sit close enough to the restaurant so they can see and only use their guns if absolutely necessary."

"They're guns? They have guns? Oh, hell no Nico. This aint no OK Corral. We gonna all go to jail. A shoot out in Robinson Township, picture that!"

"Look Rena. These dudes ain't no joke. It's not gonna lead to that but you can't go out there butt ass naked. That's stupid as hell. You gotta be prepared for the worse cuz."

"Okay, okay Nico. I gotta trust you on this one. We don't have time to argue about this. Just warn them not to get stupid. There is something else I want to talk to you about." Rena walked to the window moving back the curtains for fresh air and stealing a peek for his awaiting friends.

"Damn! You can definitely catch a contact up in here!"

"What do you need to discuss Rena. Weren't you the one worried 'bout how much time we had to get there?"

"Well, there's something I need to tell you." I'm hoping it doesn't make a difference. Anyway, I went to the bank first thing this morning and picked up a wire transfer." Rena paused.

"For? I knew you were going to take care of me. I wasn't worried 'bout the money cuz. I mean I gotta break my boys off a couple of dollars but your word has always been bond." Nico said interrupting Rena's thought.

"It's a little more than that Nico. Slim and his boys are expecting a package and I don't quite have what they're expecting?"

"What the fuck you talkin' bout Rena? You tryna get us killed? Better yet, me killed? I went out there on my word that you had they shit! What the fuck!"

"Calm down Nico. I don't have the drugs but I have fifty thousand dollars to give them instead. It's all the money I could get my hands on."

"Damn Rena! I was surprised when you said you were going to get fifty I knew a hundred wasn't gonna happen. Hold up. Let me think for a minute. Damn!"

"Nico, I know this throws things off a little. I should have told you last night when we were on the phone. I was just taken back by how fast you made the contact with Slim and I was nervous about this whole thing, I just didn't say anything."

"Well fuck it! At this point it is what it is. Fair exchange ain't no robbery. But you know now he gonna ask a whole lotta questions. Slim gonna think you got someone workin' his package and now you just tryna pay him off."

"I know. I said the same thing to Chandelle."

"What you mean like you told Chandelle? What she got to do with this? Ya'll two always up to something."

"Never mind Chandelle Nico. She was just being a good friend. She gave the money to me to pay Slim off is all. You know she had her 401k from when she quit her job. That's how she was able to afford it." Rena said trying to convince Nico so he wouldn't ask more questions about where the money came from.

"Yeah, aight Rena. I know there's more to that shit than that. Its funny Chandelle just all of a sudden left town too. Something ain't right Rena but I'm gonna leave it alone. I wish you woulda told me though up front. I coulda worked this story with Slim so we wouldn't be taking him by surprise. For your sake I hope he takes the money and keeps it movin. Otherwise, your gonna have some shit to deal with." Nico heard a horn blow. He looked at his watch and noticed that his boys were letting him to the time. They had twenty minutes to get to the restaurant.

"We gotta go Rena. We got twenty minutes. Is there anything else you wanna to tell me?" Rena checked her watch and stood up.

"No. So you're still gonna help me?"

"Yeah, Rena. I got your back. Let's go." Rena walked past Nico and out the door and down the steps to her car.

■■

Rena pulled into the Ihop parking lot and checked her rearview mirror for her cousin and his friends. Not seeing any evidence of them, she began to get nervous hoping Nico hadn't changed his mind at the last minute. *Someone please help me! How the hell do I get myself in these predicaments! I'm scared to death and Nico is nowhere to be found. What the fuck am I going to do?* Rena looked in the mirror checking her makeup when she noticed Nico walking towards the car. Rena quickly opened the car door, grabbed her purse and ran into his arms hugging him tightly.

"Damn I'm glad to see you Nico! I thought you had a change of heart." Rena said now almost in tears.

"I wouldn't leave you out here like that Rena. I walked to the restaurant from a block away. I had my boy let me out so we wouldn't be spotted together."

"That was smart. I need to trust you more Nico." Rena adjusted her dress and smoothed her hair.

"I hope the rest of this meeting goes this smoothly." He said under his breath.

"You have the money?"

"It's in the trunk. I'll get it. I was thinking about leaving it in there and if things were cool getting it later."

"No. Get it now. When we leave the restaurant we can just roll outta here."

"Give me a minute. Let me grab the bag." Rena pulled the keys from her pocket and released the lock on the trunk. Nico reached in and grabbed the bag throwing it over his left shoulder using his right hand to close the trunk and hold Renas hand.

Nico and Rena walked up the ramp to the restaurant. Nico opened the door for Rena and was greeted by the hostess. Nico whispered in Rena's ear, "I don't see Slim. Let's find a booth with a window facing the parking lot so my boys can see us."

"Can we sit at the empty booth on the left?" Rena said to the waitress walking towards the booth not chancing she'd say no.

"Sure. Please be seated and your waitress will be here in a minute to take your orders." The hostess said before walking away.

"Rena, look out the window. There he is coming up the ramp now."

"I see him. Push the bag over by me Nico. Damn, I'm nervous."

"Just chill. Remember, say as little as possible. I'm gonna get up and sit next to you and let him and his boy have this side of the booth. Their backs will be towards the door so we have a small advantage if something goes down. They won't see my boys coming."

"SShh, here he comes." Rena spoke nervously. The waitress seated Slim and his friend at the table.

"Hello lovely lady. I'm glad you were able to make it. I saw you when you pulled in the lot." Rena shifted nervously after hearing him say he was at the restaurant earlier than she thought.

"Oh, I didn't see you. Why didn't you come inside? Did you think I wouldn't show?" Nico kicked Rena softly. She looked into Nico's eyes and knew she was talking too much.

Chuckling, Slim answered. "I was just making sure you brought the bag. If you didn't have the bag well, we were going to plan B." Rena wanted to know what plan B was but didn't dare ask. She figured that she would find out his plan for her sooner or later.

Damn I'm glad I brought the bag in here with me. This motherfucker might have had me waiting in this restaurant for him until I got restless and left. He probably would've followed me back to my hotel then killed me.

"Is the package ready to go?" Slim asked looking directly at Rena. Rena looked at Nico hoping that he would say something to relieve the tension. Her stomach was in knots and she wondered if she'd make it through with her breakfast still in place.

"Is there a problem?" Slim said leaning over the table waiting for an answer.

"I have your money Slim." Rena answered reaching for the bag.

"Whatchu mean my money? " Slim said his voice growing tense. Nico stretched his arm out in front of Rena causing her to place the bag back on the floor.

"I have fifty-thousand dollars, the value of the drugs Slim. So, now we're even right?" There was a long pause at the table before Slim spoke again.

"So where are the drugs?"

"There were never any drugs Slim. None that I knew about. The police found money in the apartment and confiscated it. They didn't find any drugs and I didn't know about any until I spoke to you."

"So you are telling me that you are willing to kick out fifty g's for something you aint never have? You think I'm dumb as hell don't you?" Slim looked at Nico then turned his attention to Rena.

"I swear I'm not lying to you. I told you the other night that I didn't have the drugs and you said that if I didn't come up with them you were going to handle me. Well, this was the best I could do. I borrowed the money hoping we can call it even."

"Is that what you thought? What's up Nico. What do you know about your cousins' story? You could've got this information to me before now. You know the game. I could've put my soldiers on that package and probably double that amount with the right cut. So how do you think I should answer this?"

"Slim, I just found out about this myself. You know I don't play games. But when she told me the amount, I figured it would be cool cause it's what you were looking for in product."

"Naw son, see I got a problem now. Should I sit here and believe that she aint out here with her own crew tryna put me outta business?" Rena jumped in immediately defending herself.

"Do I look like a drug dealer to you? I aint hardly out here slinging no drugs." Rena said rolling her eyes and quickly realizing her mistake. Slim exited the booth allowing his boy to exit and stand beside Nico. Slim looked deep in Rena's eyes and without flinching instructed Nico to get up and sit on the inside of his booth.

"Nico get up real slow. We are going to exchange seats and my boy is going to sit down next you. If you get stupid, I'm gonna have to hurt your pretty cousin here." Nico got comfortable next to Rena while his friend sat down next to Nico.

"Rena, I want you to pull that bag off the floor and place it between us. Then I want to see the money inside. You understand?" Rena nodded her head doing as she was told. Placing the bag on the floor the waitress came to the table taking the order from Slim as he ordered for everyone at the table. Once the waitress left Slim directed his attention to Rena.

"Check this out baby girl. I don't know whether to believe your story or not. If you never had the package it must be nice to have that kind of money laying around. So, this is the deal. Since you have fifty gs to give out, I'm sure you can find another fifty gs to make up for my loss. See like I said, I was hoping to double that package." Rena began trembling and tears formed in her eyes.

"Slim, I swear I don't have your drugs. I didn't have the money to pay you. I got it from a girl friend of mine. I don't have any way to get another fifty thousand dollars." Rena began crying uncontrollably getting the attention of the customers in the restaurant.

"Get your shit together Rena. Stop that crying shit." Slim said dabbing her eyes with a napkin trying to downplay the seriousness of the situation.

"Look across the booth. See the gun my man has in his waistband? He's gonna use it on your cousin over there if you don't get my package or money. If you don't fix your face he won't make it outta here and we'll come get your ass later."

"Please Slim don't do this…" Before she could finish her plea the waitress came to the table with the orders.

"Miss are you okay? Is there anything I can get you?" Before Rena could answer Slim spoke.

"She'll be fine. We're family. We have a sick aunt in Ohio. Thank you." The waitress stole a quick look at Rena, nodded then walked away.

"This is what your gonna do. I'm gonna let you out and I want you to walk out of here. Don't say shit to anyone. If you do some dumb shit your cousin is dead. I watched you pull into the lot and saw Nico walk up about five minutes later. His boys drove in and parked in the back of the lot. I know this cause they never left either of those two cars back there. So you need to go out there and tell his boys to drive away or else they gonna come up missing. You got three days. You understand?"

Rena wiped her face and nodded. Slim slid out the booth and allowed Rena to walk out the door. He watched as she walked to the back of the lot and knocked on the window of the red Charger. Slim rose from the booth with Nico following him and his boy closely behind Nico. Once the Charger and Acura left the lot, Slim headed to his car. Rena watched in terror wondering once again how she was going to get out of the situation alive. Suddenly she heard a voice call out to her.

"See ya Rena baby. Don't forget three days. I'll be in touch!" Rena watched as Slim rode out the lot memorizing his license plate of his navy blue five hundred series benz.

What the fuck am I going to do? This asshole is threatening to kill Nico and I gotta come up with another fifty thousand dollars. Chandelle is going to freak and I gotta hope she didn't invest everything we have in her business venture. None of the shit we did to get this money is worth this! I gotta get back to the hotel and call Chandelle. She's gotta bring her ass here now. I can't do this shit by myself anymore. I can't handle it! Rena started her car and headed towards the 279 parkway headed to the Marriott.

Chapter 9

Chandelle checked her face quickly as she stepped from the bathroom to answer the door. Xavier was meeting her at one o'clock to take her to his office in town.

"Hello beautiful. Are you ready to go?" Xavier said helping Chandelle with her sweater.

"Yes, I'm excited about learning more about your business and looking at the new investment you were talking to me about. I'm feeling confident about all of this."

"Good. I wouldn't steer you wrong. Once you learn more about the company, our overall mission and what this means to you financially and possibly for your friends mother, I think you'll realize it's a win win situation."

"I hope so. I'm usually not so impetuous but I feel pretty comfortable. It's like I've known you for years. I don't usually jump into things like this so quickly but from what I seen so far, I believe this is a good move. The only decision I need to make at this point is exactly how much I want to invest." Xavier smiled to himself at how easy it was to convince Chandelle to have the trust of her money.

If I can get her to invest enough money, not only will I get Brian's money back but I'll have enough left over to expand my business like I always wanted to. Now I may not have to use my nest egg to take care of Brian.

"Xavier are you ready? You don't seem to be here. What are you thinking about?" Opening the door for Chandelle, Xavier said,

"I was just thinking about calling a client I was supposed to meet later this afternoon."

"We won't be all afternoon will we? You should have enough time to make your appointment."

"We won't be long at the office at all. But I have a surprise for you."

"Really? What is that?"

"The realtor called me this morning. Says she has the perfect condo for you. She said it wasn't too small and had many of the amenities you wanted even though you cut down your budget. I told her that I would take you to meet her after we left the office. She said the man who owns it is anxious to move back to the states and is willing to sell immediately. You'll be the first to see it."

"That's wonderful Xavier. Everything is moving along so much faster than I expected it to. If it's not going to cause any hardship, I'd love to see it."

"I think we can make it happen." Xavier said smiling as he handed the concierge his keys and waited for his car be brought around.

Xavier and Chandelle drove the half hour in silence except for the Monvado cd playing softly in the background. Chandelle became lost in her thoughts wondering at first why Xavier unlike any other successful Black man she had met in the past had not made any major moves on her except to tell her how beautiful she was on several occasions.

I don't know why it's bothering me that this man hasn't tried to get me in his bed. I always said I wanted a decent man who wasn't interested in getting in my panties and as soon as I meet one who is half way decent, I think something is wrong with me cause he doesn't try. I know he likes me from the looks he gives me when he thinks I'm not paying him any attention. Oh, Chandelle get it together girl. You promised yourself that you wouldn't think about getting into another relationship anytime soon especially after what went on with Derrick. Just take it slow girl. If he's worth it he won't be going anywhere any time soon. Xavier interrupted her thoughts.

"Chandelle have you had the chance to eat something this morning or would you like to stop real quick and pick something up before going to the office?"

"Yes, I mean no." Chandelle said trying to quickly process his question.

"Yes, you're hungry or no, you don't want me to stop and pick something up?"

"I'm sorry Xavier. My mind drifted a little. I was getting into the music and kinda drifted off. I was saying yes I ate this morning and no you don't have to stop for me but stop if you would like to grab something real quick." Xavier laughed.

"Movado has a way of doing that. I call it mood music." Xavier said seizing the opportunity.

"And what kind of mood is that?"

"Anytime I'm with you I'm in a romantic mood."

"Is that right?"

"Trust me." He said grabbing her hand with his free hand as he drove.

"But seriously, maybe we can get past our business early enough to grab a late lunch before we see the realtor. Or we can skip lunch all together and have dinner." Chandelle smiled just thinking about how he says all the right things especially wanting to spend all of his free time with her.

"Well, let's see how long it takes to finish our business then we can decide later."

This man really knows how to get a woman's attention. I wonder if its my money he's interested in. Mmm, I don't know. Besides, he doesn't know how much I have. I know he has clients on the daily that have five times more than I that he could have fallen in love with him if it's about money. Hel,l the man is educated, fine, and has his own business. So that can't be it. Xavier's phone rang and Chandelle watched as he fumbled trying to answer the call after checking his caller id.

"Hey Brian, what's up man?" Chandelle watched as she saw Xavier's smile slowly turned to a frown.

"Yeah man. I hear you. We had an agreement. I told you I'd take care of you. I know the date man!" Xavier said slightly raising his voice. He quickly turned his eyes from the road and glanced at Chandelle who had seemed quite shocked at Xavier's demeanor.

" Listen Brian, I'm gonna have to call you back man. I'm in the car on my way to the office and I have a client present. I'll call you back tonight." Xavier then closed his phone disconnecting the call. Xavier leaned back doing his best to regain the smooth, calm demeanor he'd maintained moments earlier.

"Xavier? Is everything okay?"

"Yeah. I'm fine. I'm so sorry about that. That was a friend of mine. He owns a restaurant on the other side of the island. He is having a charity event and I promised him that I would participate in a fund raiser he's having." Xavier said hoping to curb her curiosity.

"Are you sure? I mean you seem to have gotten upset or he was upset. Have the two of you fallen out about something?" Chandelle said wondering how a charity event could have him so uptight.

"We're fine. I just don't believe in the charity he's hosting and when I asked him to do something similar for me he signed on and on the date of the event he was a no show. It is still a sore spot for me so he thinks I'm going to not help him in retaliation."

"I see. How long have the two of you been friends?"

"Since college. I know that I need to let it go. He had a excuse but I was just trying to get my business off the ground so my event meant a lot to me."

"If the two of you have been friends that long I think you two can survive this. Friendship is something to cherish these days. We only get one or two good friends in a lifetime." Chandelle looked over at Xavier and noticed his blank stare on the roadway as if his mind was in a far away place.

"Xavier, I'm sorry. I should mind my own business. I didn't mean to pry."

"No,baby. I appreciate what you had to say. You're absolutely right. I'm gonna have to call him tonight and reassure him that I will be there." Xavier was relieved he was able to convince Chandelle that his argument wasn't anything serious but recognized her words rang of truth. He wished he'd never betrayed Brian's trust and allowed his greed to invest his best friends money when Brian said he wasn't interested.

"Well lady, we're here. My office is on the first floor of the building on your right." Chandelle turned and noticed the stucco building and was impressed by its innate beauty and architecture.

"Xavier it's simply beautiful and you have a great location. How many offices are in your building?"

"I'm its only occupant. The top floors are vacant. This part of the island is being restructured. They are trying to bring back some of the old architectural bones of many of the buildings to bring clientele to this side of the island. Many of these buildings have been vacant for the last twenty years. Now there is a renewed interest and there have been investors buying up this property like crazy. I'm hoping to own it one day and rent the top floors out to pay for the investment."

"You've chosen well for yourself. I knew you had a good eye for good investments Xavier."

"Thank you Miss Carter. I plan to do the same for you if you let me." Xavier exited the car and walked to the passenger side to help Chandelle out and walk her to his office. Xavier unlocked the door and turned on the lights and invited Chandelle to take a look around.

"Can I get you something to drink?" Xavier said heading toward a mobile bar on the right side of the spacious room.

"Yes. I'd like to have a glass of water with lemon."

"Coming right up. You don't mind if I have a glass of wine do you?"

"No. Not at all. I'm sure you can handle a glass of wine Xavier. Nice of you to ask though." Chandelle sipped from her glass and continued to admire the wall of plaques, certificates and diplomas.

"I see you are quite accomplished Xavier. Your wall is impressive." Chandelle said walking towards his desk looking at what had his attention on his laptop.

"Thank you. I've worked very hard. I like to show my clients that I am very knowledgeable when it comes to my craft. Take a look at this. I want to show you about that investment I was telling you about." Chandelle sat down in the chair facing the opposite side of his mahogany desk and began reading a memo about the new drug being introduced to help patients with diabetes.

"Xavier this sounds exciting. Do you know what this means? It sounds as if there is a cure for diabetes. How can this be so? I haven't heard a thing about this in the news. I mean this is like having a cure for cancer. How come I haven't heard about this? Except from what you've told me. I didn't then think it was this concrete. I thought it was still in the research phase. Do you know what this would mean for my friends aunt?"

"Slow down Chandelle. I know you're excited. The media doesn't even have this information yet. The FDA has yet to approve it but the pharmaceutical company is going to release its findings and go public with it as an experimental drug. The mere potential of this drug is going to make them rich just from investments. Even if it isn't approved a sizeable investment would get your desired return, you can get out and sell before there is a decision of the findings. It looks to be a pretty good investment because as you read yourself, they had eighty percent success on the lab rats tested. We can expect this to hit the market in the next few days so we'll be forced to act quickly."

"Oh my goodness! I'm so excited Xavier. The name of the company says Parker Brothers Pharmaceuticals. That's a funny name for a pharmeceutical company. Do me a favor please? Go to Yahoo finance and print out the companies history for me. I'd like to read more about it." Xavier turned the laptop on his desk took a seat and did as Chandelle requested. Xavier turned on the printer and retrieved the company bio for Chandelle to read.

"Here you go sweetheart. Tell me what you think." Chandelle took the information from Xavier and began reading the history of the company she was about to invest her future in.

Parker Brothers Pharmaceuticals was established in the U.S. in 1994. PBP began marketing FDA approved generic drugs in the U.S. in 1998 with its first approved drug Plaxca, a weight loss and water reducing dietary drug. PBP has spent the following years positioning itself as a capable player in the U.S. market with its brand and a number of generic products. The company has earned over ten billion dollars in the last five years alone. Chandelle completed the article after reading about its CEO and board of investors and how the company was projected to change the way medicine is marketed in todays economy.

"Xavier have you read this? If there is a slight possibility these projections are possible, I want to get involved with this miracle. How did you find out about this? Is this common practice? Is this how the top one percent stay rich? It just doesn't seem fair to everybody else not to have this kind of information." Xavier sat down in his chair trying to gather his words on how he was going to tell Chandelle that the information he shared with her was against the law.

"Well in complete fairness, I need to be honest with you about something. You were absolutely right when you spoke about the rich getting richer. They share this type of information amongst themselves all the time. It's the old boys' network at its best. A friend of mine keeps me informed of some of the hot commodities going on around Wall Street. He's an old friend that I helped out years ago and in turn he keeps me informed of stock trades and sells in return for some of my favorite investors who can either afford it or for my own use." Xavier said trying to read her facial expressions.

"So what you're telling me is that what he's sharing with you is secret? Is this against the law? Let me guess. Insider information right?"

"Kind of. But we're not really breaking the law because he's not telling us what to do with the information. Nor is he sharing who is investing and how much. It only become unlawful when you have information that a business is going bankrupt or breaking apart before it actually does and you act on that information by selling your stock based on that knowledge." Xavier knew he wasn't being totally truthful but was hoping that the deadline for investment was going to happen before she had the opportunity to do any investigating of her own. Chandelle's phone rang before she was able to ask Xavier another question. Chandelle checked the caller id and saw it was Rena.

"Hi. Re…"

"Chandelle!!!! We got problems!" Rena said shouting in the phone in a panic.

"Girl calm the hell down! What happened?" Chandelle looked over at Xavier raising her finger letting him know she needed a minute to finish her call. Chandelle rose from her chair and walked to the other side of the room for privacy.

"Chandelle. I went to the meeting as planned and Slim with his boy took the money and Nico with him."

"What?!!" Chandelle said realizing she yelled and quickly turned facing Xavier and smiled to play off the horror in her voice.

"Xavier can you ecuse me for a minute? I need to step outside and take this call." Xavier nodded is head in understanding but continued to stare until she was out of sight outside behind the door.

"Okay Rena. Now go slow and tell me what happened."

"Chandelle our worst fears came true. Nico and I went to the meeting and I told Slim that I had fifty thousand dollars to pay him for the drugs. Well, he didn't believe that I didn't have the drugs and thinks I'm out selling them and the fifty thousand was just payment from the drugs I'm dealing on the streets. I told him I never knew where the drugs were and hoped that he would be happy with the money. He said that if I was able to come up with fifty thousand then I could come up with another fifty." Chandelle listened intently and began pacing back and forth trying to think of a way out of the mess they were in.

"Didn't you tell him that the money was loaned to you?"

"Yeah, I told him. He said if you had fifty to loan you could afford to loan fifty more. He said he planned on putting a cut on the drugs and doubling up. And the bottom line is he wants his drugs or the money.

"How long did he give you to come up with the money?"

"He said a week. The same amount of time he gave me the first time. I wish we didn't pay him so quickly and waited out the full week. Now he thinks I just have money laying around. Girl, I wish we would have left those drugs for the police to find then we wouldn't be in this mess. It's not worth it." Rena said starting to cry all over again.

"Get a grip Rena! Can't cry about it now. We could've done a lot of things differently but we didn't. You know as well as I did that we took it for a future nest egg. Your mom who I love dearly just got out the hospital and we have another huge hospital bill to pay. We have been tearing our savings up getting her the best of care."

"So what are you trying to say? If it wasn't for my…"

"Shut the hell up Rena! I'm not putting this on you or your mom. I love you both and would do anything for the two of you. You know that! We knew we didn't have enough money to live without a hustle or a job. That's why we planned on opening our own business to make more money. We knew our cut wasn't going to take care of us forever."

"I know Chandelle. I'm sorry. I'm just scared. We don't have long to come up with something. He said he's going to kill Nico if he doesn't get his money. He also said he was going to kill me. I'm still at the hotel but I only have a week before he finds me. He probably knows where I am but he's going to give me the week to get his money."

"Shit Rena. So you think he's in town? I remembered you said something about him not being from Pittsburgh."

"I think so because Nico was able to get to him quick. He didn't contact Slim directly but he met with us the following day. So, I think he's still here. Plus I think he's gonna try to find out if there is a new supplier on the streets to see if I was lying to him. Now that Ricky is dead all the guys on the streets that were working for Ricky now work for Slim. He was

Ricky's supplier remember? He's gotta stick around to get his business straight right?"

"I guess so. But Rena you're scaring me now. You sure do know a lot about street hustling."

"I lived with one remember? I ain't stupid. I had to keep up with what crazy ass Ricky was doing plus Nico always let me know what was going on in the street."

"Damn this is going to cut into my plans here if I send you another fifty thousand dollars."

"Chandelle I don't think it's smart to send me the money anyway. He's not going to do anything but try to get more. I was dealing with his dead partner. There is no way that he's going to just walk away. He's gonna swear I was cutting money from the top from Ricky and probably thinks its rightfully his."

"So what are you saying Rena?" Chandelle said surprised that Rena was using her head despite the stress. She was used to being the one to come up with both the plans and ideas.

"Chandelle you need to get on a plane to Pittsburgh tonight."

"Tonight? I can't get a plane tonight! What is that going to prove anyway?"

"First of all, I'm tired of being in this shit by myself while you are soaking up the sun and house shopping all day. I need you here. Besides as long as you're here you can always transfer the money if you need to once you get here. Girl, we gotta revert to our back in the day shit and get in the streets."

"And do what? We have'nt been in the streets in years. We don't know anybody anymore. The streets are for these young kids not some old played out wanna bees.

"You know what they say. The streets don't change just the players. I know some of Ricky's hustlers and I met a couple of Nico's friends today. His friends followed us to the meeting were spotted by Slim but they can get us some information I'm sure. I owe Nico. I would never forgive myself if something happened to him. There is nothing to say that they would be satisfied with killing him and decide to come after me and anybody who knows me."

"Okay Rena. I'm going to get a flight there first thing tomorrow morning. Ill call you with the details on the flight and you can meet me at the airport. I have to tie up some loose ends here tonight though."

"Loose ends? What are you up to? You didn't get us a place yet did you?"

"I'm suppose to go look at one today but I'm not going to commit to anything until we clear this situation up first. But remember I was telling you about the other investment that could make us some money?" Chandelle said excited about making up for their loss to Slim.

"Yes, what about it?" Rena said.

"Well it presented itself today. Girl some pharmaceutical company came up with a cure for diabetes."

"Huh? How come my mother doesn't know anything about this? We are paying top dollar for her care. She's on this shit everyday. You know how guilty she feels about us paying for her care. She still doesn't know that she's not covered by insurance and we are paying cash."

"I'll explain it to you later. It's a long story but it's exciting. Do you know how much money we can make from this deal? We may never have to work again another day in our life after this one."

"Oh shit. Here we go again. Chandelle if sounds too good to be true it usually is. Why the hell would anyone tell a nobody like your ass about the invest of a lifetime and no one else knows about it? Your sex ain't that damn good" Rena said chuckling for the first time in days.

"Fuck you Rena. I'm not sleeping with him but his name is Xavier. I just happened to be in the right place at the right time. Besides he shared some information with me that I'm sure he doesn't want me to repeat so he has to be on the up and up. I haven't led you wrong so far have I?"

"Well, I'm not going to say you led me wrong because I'm a big girl and I make my own decisions but I will say I wish we would've done things a little differently."

"Look Rena, I'll call you tonight with my flight information okay?

"Okay. Talk to you later. Love you." Chandelle closed her phone and made her way back to the office and opened the door to find Xavier's head buried in his laptop.

"I'm sorry that took so long." Chandelle said as she sat in the leather chair opposite him.

"It's fine. I understand things happen. I guess now it's my turn to ask you if everything is okay." Xavier asked with sincere concern in his eyes.

"I'm fine. Remember my best friend I told you about? The one who is like a sister to me? That was her on the phone. She was giving me an update on her mother. She had some misinformation from one of the nurses at the hospital and we had to get a doctor on the phone to clarify a few things. That girl almost had me thinking that her mom was on her deathbed. But I do need to leave for Pittsburgh in the morning." Xavier's eyebrows rose in shock over the news that she was leaving town and he was going to miss out on his lottery winnings.

"I thought you said it wasn't as serious as she first explained it. Her mom was going to be fine." Xavier said knowing he wasn't going to be able to convince her to stay.

"She's not dying but they are going to have to perform a serious procedure tomorrow and I really need to be there."

"When do you expect to be back? I understand your leaving but I just wanted to remind you that we don't have time on this investment. If we prolong this by the time you get back the stock price per share is going to be out of our league and not worth the investment. I was hoping we could tie this up by tomorrow." Chandelle listened carefully to what Xavier quickly decided to risk the investment and hope that her money would double by the time she got back. She would make a decision if she wanted to continue the investment she got back.

Fuck! I gotta get Brian's half mil back to him and I only have a couple of weeks to get it to him. I got to get this money from her and get it tonight.

"Xavier, I usually don't do things like this without doing some homework but I'm going to take a chance on your character and I'm a pretty good judge of character, and do this."

Yes! My game is the shit! I can have a half mil for Brian and do almost equally as well for myself. Okay Xavier stay cool brother. Don't look too happy or anxious. Convince her she made a good decision.

"I think you've made a good decision Chandelle. You're about to be a very wealthy woman. You don't have to worry about meeting the realtor this afternoon. I know you have plans to make. Leave everything to me."

"Yes. You're right. I almost forgot about her. Please call her with my apologies and assure her that I will be in touch when I get back. So how do we do this? Check or cash?

"How bout we meet in the middle of the road and go to the bank for a cashiers check?"

"That's fine." Chandelle said grabbing her purse to get ready to leave.

"Good. We can take care of the cashier check at the bank and while we are waiting to meet with the bank manager we can make sure you have all my contact information in case you need me while you're out of town."

Damn! I need to find a bank manager somewhere. If I'm not getting friendly with anybody else they're sure getting to know me. Chandelle thought to herself then sighed.

Chapter 10

Chandelle sat back comfortably on the jet reminiscing on how she got in her current predicament. Just weeks ago she'd been on a similar plane believing she was headed towards the life she had always dreamed of.

I never thought I would be on my way back to Pittsburgh this soon. Just months ago I had the perfect plan of robbing a casino. Everything was perfect. I don't know what Rena had planned but I'm not trying to get hurt over some damn drugs. Rena needs to consider just paying that clown off, getting her cousin home safe, then getting her packed and out of Pittsburgh. Slim and his side- kick, are small-time hoods and I doubt that they would follow us to the island. Only thing I need to do is call Xavier tomorrow . I just wanna move on with my life. Chandelle heard the overhead ding allowing her to unhook her seatbelt and roam the cabin freely. Chandelle saw a stewardess heading her way.

"Excuse me miss? May I have a bottle of water please?"

"Yes. We will be coming through the cabin shortly offering refreshments."

"Thanks. Can you bring a pillow too?

"Sure. I would be happy to get that for you." Chandelle retrieved the pillow from the stewardess and decided to nap until she reached Pittsburgh. She was tired of replaying everything had been going on in her life in the past months. All of her dreams of success and fortune were quickly becoming a nightmare and without a solution to her distress sleep was the only thing at the moment that could give her peace and relieve her of the stress.

■■

Rena gathered the rest of her things together and threw them in her overnight bag. *I still have a couple of hours before I have to meet Chandelle. Let me make some calls before I set up a meeting then, pick her up to meet with whoever, then find us a room that's a little more low key so we can put together a viable plan. Let me call Smid now. He was Rickys runner and they'd been known to double date on occasion. Ricky always said it was good business to go out with the boys in order to have the allegiance of your workers. I never wanted to be bothered with any of his ghetto friends but now I'm so glad I did. He may be able to help us or tell us who can. Where's my damn phone!* Rena pulled the covers back and noticed the phone lying next to the pillow. She pressed the button for her contacts and scrolled till she reached Keisha's number and prayed that Smid was home. Rena hadn't heard from him since Ricky's death. She doubted that she would hear from him ever again. Rena dialed the number and listened for someone to pick up the phone.

"Hello?"

"Hi. This is Rena. Is Smid home?"

"Hey Rena. This is Smid. What's up witcha you baby girl? I never thought I'd hear from you again."

"Hey Smid. I thought that was you. I'm good. How are you?"

"I'm straight. Keisha isn't here right now. You need me to leave her a message?"

"No. Actually, I'm glad you answered the phone cause I really needed to talk to you. I'm in a bit of trouble and I kinda need your help."

"Whassup?"

"Well, I met Slim. You know who he is right?" Rena said trying to be careful about what she said over the phone.

"Yeah. I know who he is. What is up?"

"He thinks I'm mixed up in Ricky's dealings and he has something that belongs to me. Well, not really belonging to me but something like that. Anyway, I need your help. I need you to tell me what to do. I have no one else to turn to."

"Damn Rena. I really don't want to fuck wit that dude. I'm not even working for him. I heard he came to town after Ricky died and took over. I'm doing my own shit. I don't know how I can help you…" Rena quickly cut Smid off.

"Smid, I don't want to get into this over the phone. Listen, I have to pick my girlfriend up from the airport this afternoon.

Can she and I meet you a little later so we can sit down and talk?"

"Rena, Ricky was my boy and I'm going to meet you on the strength of him but I can't promise you that I can do anything for you. What time you talking?"

"How bout four o'clock? I'll meet you down at Art's for a couple of drinks. We can talk and it won't be that crowded at that time and we can talk."

"Bet. I'll be there."

"Thanks Smid." Rena hung up the phone, grabbed her luggage and purse and headed for the airport.

■■■

Rena smiled as she watched Chandelle walk from the terminal with her luggage in tow.

"Chandelle, You don't know how glad I am to see you." Rena grabbed Chandelle around the neck and hugged her tightly not wanting to let her go.

"Okay, Rena I'm glad to see you too." She said pulling Rena's arms from her neck.

"You can let me go now." Chandelle said laughing at her friends' theatrics. "Rena, trust me everything is going to be fine. We are going to fix this and everything is going to be okay. Lets get to the car. Were you able to contact anybody?"

"Yeah." Rena said as she grabbed Chandelles bags and walked out the airport towards the lot.

"We're to meet him at Art's at four. We have about twenty minutes to get there. We may as well meet him first then figure out where we are going to stay later."

"Did you check out your hotel?"

"Yeah. I think we should stay somewhere a little low key. Plus, I paid with a credit card. Unless they're following me, I don't want them to find us." Rena started the engine and the sounds of Maxwell filled the car.

"We should stay somewhere on the East Side. You know those raggedy hotels over there don't ask for id when you check in and you can get those rooms by the hour if you want to." Chandelle took a moment and stared at Rena in amazement.

"There you go again. Girl, you're watching too many damn movies. These dudes ain't that deep. They're nothing but some nickel dime hustlers from Steubenville."

"Whatever! There are some serious gangsters in Steubenville. I'm not taking any chances. They have my cousin and it's not going to hurt being careful."

"Okay Rena. We'll do it your way. I can't wait till this shit is over with. Speaking of which, I need to make a phone call. I went ahead and made that investment I was telling you about."

"What? That was quick Chandelle. Are you sure you did the right thing? How much did you invest?"

"Almost all of it." Chandelle said turning to look at the scenery out the passenger side window. She knew Rena was about to lose her mind but she was ready to stand by her decision if she had to.

"Now who watches too much TV? Your investment sounded too good to be true and it probably is. But Chandelle you always did do your homework but I've never seen you jump into something so quickly." There was a eerie silence and when Chandelle didn't say anything she took her eyes off the rode and looked at Chandelle.

"Chandelle did you sleep with him? Is this what this is about? He gave you some good- good and you lost your mind?"

"No Rena I didn't sleep with him. In fact he has been nothing but a gentleman."

"Well then, why did you do it?"

"I have to admit it was a little emotional but I did get a chance to check him out. I went to his job, met his friends and even visited his office. He's good, he's professional and he's successful Rena. He didn't get there by making bad investments."

"I hear ya, I hope you know what you are doing. That is our dream you're messing with. But you know what? I'm not going to say shit cause at this point I just want this shit to go away and have my life back. Shit we robbed a casino and got paid. I trust you girl in whatever you do." Rena pulled into Art's parking lot ready to have a few drinks to calm her nerves. Chandelle got out the car and thought back at the nights she spent in Art's with her girls getting tore up then looking for an after hours joint to go dancing till five or six in the morning before heading home.

Damn this place brings back some memories. I've met some fine honeys up in this place back in the day. First few years we didn't have any business in here. We were hardly old enough to vote. Chandelle laughed to herself as she reached the door taking in the familiar atmosphere. *Damn this place hasn't changed a bit. A couple of new stools but this place still looks the same.*

"Chandelle, come on, Smid is sitting across the bar." Rena and Chandelle easily made their way to the other side of the bar and pulled up a chair.

"Hey, Smid. Thanks for meeting me."

"I thought I was just meeting you. Who is your girl with you?"

"Oh, this is my best friend, Chandelle. She's cool. I wanted her here to listen in."

"I ain't makin' no promises Rena. What you need?" Smid said taking a swallow from his Heineken.

"Slim came in town as you know because of what happened to Ricky." Rena still has yet to come to terms with Ricky's death because she knew she was the cause by killing him. She knew that if that information ever got out she could fall under the same fate. Rena called over the bartender to order drinks for her and Chandelle giving her time to get her story together.

"I still don't know what that has to do with you Rena. I been thinking bout this all day since you called me. I even made a couple calls to see what's happenin' in the streets."

"What did you find out?" Rena said anxious to hear any news about her cousin.

"Nothin' that made any sense. Talk to me and let me see if anything makes sense."

"Well, Slim heard that after Ricky got shot they found some money in the apartment. They claimed that they left a package with Ricky and they think I have it or know where it is."

"Word? And? They want you to get them the package?"

"Exactly. But Smid you know Ricky didn't have me in his business like that. I don't know nothing bout any drug package. Slim is saying it was worth fifty thousand dollars and he was hoping to make at least double that on the street."

"I know you told him that. So what he say?"

"Yes, I told me that. That's where my girl comes in. I called her and she loaned me the money to pay him. I figured that id I gave him the money he would leave me alone."

"Tell me you didn't give that motha fucka fifty g's."

"I did. You know my cousin Nico right?" Smid shook his yes while taking another long sip from the bottle.

"Well, he went with me while a couple of his boys sat in the parking lot and watched out for us."

"And?" Smid said as if waiting for the punch line of a bad joke.

"He said he didn't believe that I didn't have the drugs. He figures that if I had fifty g's to pay him off I could either get another fifty g's and I was working the package. He gave me a week to come up with the money or the package and said if I don't come up with it Nico was through then he was coming after me."

"Damn Rena. That's fucked up. You are in some shit. I wish you would have called me first before making that move."

"I went to Nico cause he's family and he usually knows what's going on in the street. What would have you done differently?" Rena said sipping her drink.

" It doesn't matter baby girl. Who knows it could be me on lockdown with Slim instead of Nico. But some of this shit is making sense now."

"Like what Smid?"

"I called E to see what was up down the way. I don't know if you know him or not."

"No. I don't think so." Rena said.

"He worked for Ricky and stayed on with the crew. He said word came down that he and the rest of the crew were told to chill."

"Did he say why?" Chandelle who didn't say anything through the entire conversation chimed in.

"Hush Rena. Let the man finish. Quit asking so many questions." Rena looked at Chandelle and rolled her eyes.

"I thought it was cause the streets were hot at first but after listening to your story it makes some sense. Slim is probably trying to see if the junkies are still getting served. There's only a couple of us he allows us to hustle cause he knows we ain't no threat. This way he can see if there is any new shit in the streets. I was pretty much advised to stay off the streets too. I said hell naw cause I gotta eat." Smid looked at Rena to see if she understood before continuing.

"So, What are you gonna do Smid? I'm paying for any help you can provide."

"I'll go on the block tonight to see what I can find out. Since nobody's working I know somebody's willing to talk. Niggas are willing to talk if they hungry enough and paid the right amount of money. Just keep your cell phone on and I'll hit you up tonight when I find something out."

"Thank you so much Smid. I don't know how I can repay you for this." Rena said.

"Ricky was my man. I don't mind looking out for his woman. I know he would do it for me. Besides, I don't like that nigga Slim. That's why I aint working for him now. He's shady as hell." Smid threw back the remainder of his beer and left a tip for the waitress. Rena and Chandelle watched as he left the bar.

"So what now Dick Tracy?" Chandelle said in jest.

"Very funny Chandelle. We might as well get out of here and grab something to eat and a place to stay until Smid calls. I guess we'll play it by ear from there."

Chapter 11

Xavier went to his guest bedroom and pulled his luggage from the top of his closet. He searched the bottom looking for his Nikes and jackets to take on his upcoming trip to New York.

I know it's chilly in New York this time of year but I may have to stay and chill out for a while before heading back here. Maybe I should take a coat just in case. Xavier quickly packed his bags in an attempt to make the eight o'clock red eye leaving for New York. He had wired the money given to him by Chandelle earlier that morning and he wanted to be close to the exchange in the morning when Wall Street opened.

By closing tomorrow I should have enough money to pay my boy Brian his funds and the fees to Charles Coleman for brokerage fees. If it flips like he has it projected, I will be a very wealthy man by this time tomorrow night. I truly wish things didn't have to go down like this. I really liked Chandelle. She could've been Mrs. Barnes. Maybe she still can. *Oh well, I can't worry about that now. I'm going to send her a letter and let her know that she lost her money in the market and I can't face her knowing how much this deal meant to her. Shit, she knew the risk.* Xavier carried his luggage to the door. *Okay, I think I got everything. I just need to call the office and let the boss know I need a few days. I'll make up some lie about a sick aunt I need to go see and need time off. If he has problems with it, fuck him. I only need him for the benefits anyway. I'll have enough money to let him know I quit anyway. I'd quit now but I need to see my money first in case something happens to go wrong.* Xavier pulled his phone from his pocket and called the office to speak to his boss.

"Morton and Meyers brokerage firm, Micheal Richards speaking can I help you?"

"Hey Micheal, this is Xavier. What's up man? Is Mr. Meyers around?"

"Hey Xavier. No he left for the day. Didn't you see what time it is?"

"Yeah. You know how he stays around the office late some nights looking at the days numbers. He's working trying to sew up any loose ends. You know that." Xavier said laughing into the phone.

"What are you still doing there man?"

"I need clients man. I'm answering the phones for the stragglers. You wouldn't know anything bout this." Micheal said jokingly but truthfully telling it like it was. Xavier's success was no secret and everyone envied the fact that he had enough overflow of clients to start a side business of his own.

"Aw man if I had your bank account I would'nt have to work anymore." Xavier said trying to lighten the mood.

"I was calling cause I need to take some time off. I have to go to new York for a week or two on some personal business and was just calling to let him know."

"Oh, I'm sorry to hear about that man. How long do you think you'll be gone?"

"I don't know. I'll be there at least until I get everything in order. Like I said, it may take a week or two. I'm the only one who is able to call off right now. I'm glad I saved up those vacation days."

"I hear you man. Damn, I know you hate leaving that fine woman you had in here the other day. How is that working out anyway?"

Damn I forgot he met Chandelle that quickly. He's always on my shit when it comes to a woman. I can't wait till some woman gives him the time of day so he can quit living my life.

"She's straight. I told her that when I get settled I would invite her up. Anyway, Mike I gotta go. I gotta a plane to catch. I'll let Meyers know and see you when I get back." Xavier said disconnecting the call without hearing Mike say goodbye. Xavier called his boss and left a message. He then made sure all the lights were turned off in the condo and headed to his car for the airport.

■■

Rena heard her phone ringing on the side table by her bed. She looked at the clock and saw that it was two in the morning. She grabbed her phone knowing immediately who was calling her at that hour.

"Hello?"

"Hey Rena, it's Smid. Sorry it's late but you told me to call you as soon as I heard something." Rena sat up straight in the bed and looked across the room to see if Chandelle was awakened by the call. They decided it was safer to stay together in the same room just in case something happened. At least Rena thought it was safer and as tired as Chandelle was she wasn't in any mood to argue.

"I'm glad you called Smid. What did you hear?"

"I was right about Slim. He got the workers off the block to see if you were working the streets. Nobody is happy about it either. Anyway, I found out where they are staying. I think your cousin is with them too because a couple of the fellas paid him a visit and his boy was posted up at the door and wouldn't let

them in. They said they think something is about to go down cause Slim was talking business to them in the street and that's not how he operates. They said he never even wants to be seen around them let alone talk business and risk being overheard. They gettin' nervous cause they thinkin' there is either going to be a take over by someone else moving in cause they aint workin' or his boys in Steubenville are going to come to town and replace them."

"So you didn't tell them what's up?" Rena asked.

"Not really. But I did put some feelers out to find out who would be willing to put some work in. I figured that if you were payin you could get some back up for the right price. These niggas is starvin' and they don't give a fuck bout no Slim."

"Anything's better than trying to come up with fifty g's. he can't get the package cause I don't have it. Now all I need is a plan."

"I hear ya. Let me find out how many soldiers I can recruit and go check out where he's staying so we can get in and out with your cousin hopefully without anyone getting hurt."

"Thanks again Smid. Remember I only have a week and I'm now down to five days. I don't want to wait till the deadline cause he's going to get nervous or be expecting me to do something out of desperation. I got to catch him when he least suspects it."

"I hear you baby girl. Get some sleep. You should hear from me later this evening or early tomorrow. I'll have a price tag and plan for you, which should give you enough time to get your funds together."

"Okay Smid. I'll talk to you then. Be safe." Rena closed her phone and stared at the phone revisiting the conversation she had with Smid.

"Rena, are you okay?" Rena snapped out of her trance giving her attention to Chandelle who was awake and staring at her quizzically.

"Yeah, I'm fine. Did the phone wake you up?"

"No. Not really. I haven't been sleeping lately." Chandelle said rearranging the blankets on her bed.

"What do you mean? What's wrong?"

"I've been having this recurring dream about being tried for the casino robbery and murder."

"Damn Chandelle, I didn't know you were having problems over what we did. You have to let it go. Besides, Ricky was going to be tried for the murder before they found him dead."

"I know Rena but none of it would've happened if I didn't come up with the plan in the first place."

"Chandelle, look at the good that has come out of it. Two of our best friends are living out their dreams, which wouldn't have been possible if it hadn't been for you. My mother is probably still alive because of the money we have that is paying her medical bills."

"I hear you girlfriend. I appreciate what you're saying. We just got to get past this situation and then I think I'll be alright. If not, I think I got enough money for a shrink." Chandelle said chuckling trying to make light of the situation. Rena smiled reassuringly.

"Listen, I just got off the phone with Smid. He called to give me the skinny."

"And?"

"Aint nothing really. I'll tell you about it in the morning. Get some sleep. I know you're tired from the trip and running around we did today. I'm beat. I haven't slept in days but Smid relieved some of my stress so maybe I can get a couple of hours."

"Okay. Let's talk in the morning. I need to get up early and make some phone calls. Wake me up if you get up before I do." Chandelle watched as Rena turned off the light above the side table and pulled the blankets up over her head.

Chapter 12

Ding! Ding! Ding! Xavier's heart did a flip flop hearing the bell indicating the opening of trading on Wall Street.

Damn! Every time I hear that sound I get excited. This is where I need to be. If I had the same opportunity here I could've made the money I'd been looking for a couple of years ago. Some of these guys are making close to a million dollars a year if you add in some of the perks they get and they don't have my drive and knowledge. There's my boy Charles walking across the floor with some of the powerful players in New York. Damn if that shouldn't be me.

Xavier watched Charles converse with the man he'd recognized as the CEO of the pharmaceutical company he just invested Chandelles money with. Charles looked up acknowledging Xavier then quickly turned his attention back to his conversation. Xavier watched the ticker tape on the far wall and watched as PBP 5k @20.01 ^ 0.001 crept across the board.

Parker Brothers Pharmaceuticals was trading a penny above the initial investment of twenty dollars a share he paid Charles.

Well, it's on now. I haven't been here twenty minutes and I just earned five hundred dollars. If it continues at this rate... Damn, I can't even do the math right now. Xavier watched for the tape to go around and check the rate on the next go around. *Fuck! The taped jumped alphabetically from N to R. PBP didn't show. Okay, don't panic Xavier. Charles assured me that there were more than fifty thousand shares invested. I invested that much myself. Anything fifty thousand and under has a slow trading display and 50k aren't enough shares to make investors excited and buy. But on the other hand it may be trading high and the ticker isn't keeping up with the investments being made. Be patient Xavier just be patient. Here it comes again, PBP 10k @40.00 ^ 2.0. Yes! I doubled my money.* Xavier grinned before searching the floor again. Charles was watching Xavier's reaction. Charles nodded and gave Xavier the thumbs up sign. For the next four hours Xavier watched the tape and made small talk with a couple of traders on the floor but never letting his eyes leave his investment slowly increasing in shares but he was content that he more than doubled his money by two o'clock. *Two more hours to go and I can walk outta here a very happy man.* At three the floor was still active with brokers screaming and answering phones trying to get the best deals offered. Suddenly, an eerie silence crept across the floor that lasted barely a minute but seemed like hours because of the noise. Xavier watched as the tape which was lit in a holiday green displaying the gains of the day suddenly blinked red taking a nose dive and PBP with it. Xavier saw his two million- dollar investment that rose to four and a half million- fall off by fifty thousand dollars in less than a minute. Xavier frantically searched the floor for Charles who turned suddenly towards him and raise his hand to cool Xavier's fears. Xavier instantly went into panic mode but didn't grab his phone to make the call to sell off his shares. His experience taught him that pulling his shares could be a major mistake and knew that a recovery could be instantaneous. He also knew the risk that pulling out early would hurt the investment. He and Charles had a gentlemen's agreement..

Their agreement was that he couldn't sell until instructed by Charles and then and only then could he collect or face a penalty and a major fee of sixty percent for an early withdrawal. That penalty alone could put him in a position of having less money than when he started.

■■■

"Hurry up Chandelle!" We're running late. Smid is waiting for us!"

Chandelle closed her cell phone and pulled her overnight bag on her shoulder as she walked out the hotel door.

"Get in the car. Why do you have that crazy look on your face? Rena said giving Chandelle a quick glance before pulling the sky blue Sonata into midday traffic.

"I tried calling Xavier and his phone went straight to voice mail."

"It's early Chandelle. Just call him later. Did you leave him a message?"

"Yes, but I called him yesterday when I first got here and he didn't answer. He was making the investment yesterday and I haven't heard from him since."

"Let it go for now Chandelle. Let's get through this first then we can talk about your boy. We gotta stay focused." Chandelle nodded then kept her focus out her side window reading the overhead signs above the highway wondering where they were headed.

"If your wondering, we're meeting Smid at the at the Eat N' Park in the Rocks. Chandelle half listened to Rena knowing in her gut that something wasn't right with Xavier. *If Xavier fucked me over, I won't have to worry bout dreaming of court cause I'm going to jail for real. I swear I'll kill his punk ass. Smooth talkin' Jamaican, meat patty eatin', son-of-a bitch.*

"Snap the hell out of it Chandelle. We're here. C'mon and get out. I can see Smid from here." Rena and Chandelle walked inside and were greeted by the hostess who showed them to the booth where Smid was seated.

"Hey Smid. I hope you weren't waiting long."

"Naw, I'm cool but time is of the essence. We gotta get this together cause we don't have a lot of time and nico's life is at stake." Rena looked at Chandelle who wasn't giving Smid her full attention decided to speak for the both of them.

"Okay Smid what's up?"

"Your cousin is being held in a warehouse down in the bottoms. Slim had his street runners delivering food at night. One of my boys I worked the corners with took the trip to the warehouse." Tears began to roll down Rena's cheeks. She raised her left hand to wipe her face then exhaled.

"Since your boy knows where Nico is being held, is your friend willing to help us?" Rena asked starting to get anxious.

"Naw but he let me know that he was told to use the same entrance both times. He was able to give me a good description of the inside of the warehouse and said Nico's okay and said he's bound and gagged to a chair in the middle of the floor."

"What the hell is that all about? Why wouldn't he hide Nico? He trusted his boys that much not to say anything?"

"Guess he figures if there's a snitch he'd be dealt with but I'm figuring he's sending a message to his crew that he's not to be fucked with. Ricky was thorough and had the crews respect but word on the street was he was going to get tried if he got any bigger in the game cause the streets thought he was soft. I think my boy was just smart." *You right about that. Ricky wasn't going to give anyone a chance to try him cause his plan was to take his drug money and the money he stole from Chandelle and skip town before the shit got any thicker.* Rena thought to herself.

"I got young brothas who are tryin to come up are going to help us get your cousin back as long as you willin' to pay. You lookin at bout ten g's to get this handled." Slim said.

"No problem. I gotcha." Rena looked over at Chandelle to see if there would be a problem paying. Chandelle nodded her head in agreement and Rena continued,

"When will we know for sure?"

"Here comes my young buck now." Rena and Chandelle turned around and watched as the young man Polo'd down from head to toe approached the table. Rena watched as the young man situated his baseball hat tilting it to the side of his head. He couldn't be any older than about nineteen or twenty with tattoos covering his body. Her eyes fixated on the one that said thug on one side of his neck and life on the other. She wondered if he could ever have a future in front of him besides the one he was living now. Nodding his head in acknowledgement to Rena and Chandelle he sat down in the booth next to Smid.

"Yo, Smid I got that info for you if you ready man." He said looking at Smid making sure it was okay to speak the plan in front of company.

"You straight. This is Rena and Chandelle." Smid said giving introductions.

"Wassup queens." Rena and Chandelle said hello in unison while he continued.

"Check it out. I spoke to a couple of my boys and dey down for whateva. I went over to da East side and politicked wit dese niggas who said dey wit it if the money's straight. I told dem bout dem numbers we talked bout earlier. No whatta mean? Dey was cool cause you know dey tryna control da West Side anyway. No whatta mean? Dey see dis as a oppo'tunity to take over. I let dem know though dey had to handle dat shit later cause we on another tip. I'm figurin' five of us gone do the damn thing up right.

"Cool. I think we have enough power to go in there tonight. How you packin' son?"

"C'mon Smid! You know how we roll! Nothin' extreme, couple of uzi's and a glock. Yo boy said dere was only four soldiers and yo man locked up. We usually roll deep but just so as not to arouse suspicion aint but four of us gonna hit the spot. We should be able to take dem down soon as we hit the door."

Rena's eyes widened when she realized a wild west show was about to go down.

"Um, Smid. I understand the guns are necessary but I want to make sure my cousin doesn't get hurt. I also don't want to be on tomorrows six o'clock news. We gotta come up with something a little cleaner than going in and shooting up the place." Chandelle shook her head in agreement then finally spoke.

"I think we should wait until they call out for food tonight. You said that he calls out every night so when the delivery comes we could go in behind him."

Ignoring Chandelle, the young man known only as Black continued,

"I know Nico. He's a good brotha but my uzi don't know that. If I go in there with a full clip and have to start sprayin', there's a good chance he could catch one. You know if we roll deep and try to house dem niggas they gonna suspect something. So, what's the plan? How you wanna handle dis?"

"Check it out. We gonna park down from the warehouse so we can have full view but far enough away nobody is gonna notice us. I know most of the runners workin for Slim so when I see somebody going in the warehouse that's when we gonna make our move. There's only two ways in the warehouse that can be used. It's been empty for years so all the doors to the loading dock are rusted and can't be opened. There is a door on Linton they usin' to get in and out that doesn't raise any suspicion and a steel dock door in the back that can be used but would draw too much attention. Slim and his boy got their trucks parked in the back by that door. All the windows in the place have been covered with two by fours so we aint gotta worry bout nobody on the street seeing what's going on inside. Ya'll wit me so far?" Smid asked looking around the table. Everybody nodded and waited for him to continue with the plan.

"Once we go in Black, you and your boy position your guns on Slim's soldiers. His right hand man will no doubt be at his side and the other two will probably be close to Nico. There's a TV up in that joint and they waitin' on their food so they'll probably be looking at the tube on the small table next to Nico waitin for the delivery. If you gotta take one or both of them out as an example, do the damn thing. Once the place is secure, I'll go to the door to let Rena and Chandelle in to handle they business. You a'ight with that ladies?" Rena was the first to speak.

"I don't have a problem with that. Once we go in though, I want my cousin untied and taken to one of the cars outside. Slim shouldn't be a problem cause his boys will be either covered or dead. I don't want to have to worry bout my back and his."

"I hear you. Once you pay this nigga we can cover you and we'll be out." Rena shook her head in agreement.

"Rena, I hope you know what you're doin. Once you pay this nigga, you know he may come back for more don't you?"

"I know but I'm planning for this to be my last stand then I'm outta here. Besides, what choice do I have? I can't kill him and I can't afford the cost to have you do it."

"Yeah, its gonna cost you bout five times more than agreed upon but when it's done you won't have to worry bout it no more." Rena looked at Chandelle giving her a look that asked if they could afford. Chandelle knew that killing Slim was the best option but she didn't have enough money to pay and have the job done.

I'm not planning to pay Slim his fifty grand either. I can't afford to lose this money to some wanna be gangsta on the street. I haven't heard from Xavier and I gave him all of our money and my gut tells me something ain't right. I can't take the chance.

"I tell you what we can do. Before we go into the warehouse we'll gas the place so once we leave out we'll blaze it. If we're lucky dem motha fuckas will go up with the place. The po- po will blame dem for the place goin' up. Ain't nobody gonna investigate the shit once the coroner identifies the bodies and they find out its some drug dealers. It'll look like a drug deal gone bad." Chandelle smiled lightly hoping that the plan might work.

"We gone meet back here round ten. They order when the places are about to close. If anything goes wrong we'll meet back here tomorrow. Slim would never come back to the Rocks lookin or askin' questions if he makes it out. I'll meet Black at the usual spot to get paid. Go out and school your boys and I'll check you later." Smid's soldier got up twisting his cap to the back and walked towards the door. Rena stood and hugged Smid's hand thanking him before whispering to Chandelle,

"I think this might work Chandelle."

"I hope so Rena. I really do.

Chapter 13

Xavier woke up to the sound of his phone. He grabbed his cell from his pants pocket laying on the footstool at the bottom of the bed.

Damn! It's Chandelle again. I had plans on calling her yesterday after the closing of the bell to give myself time to get back to the islands, settle my affairs then disappear before she returned from Pittsburgh. Instead, I'm stuck here in New York trying to even my score with Charles. Why did he have to pick this deal for me to return the favor? I knew I would have to even the score one day but I was hoping it would be somewhere down the road. He made money from this just like I did. I can't imagine what he wants from me in return. Xavier again replayed the conversation he had with Charles before he left the exchange floor looking for clues to what couldn't be in store for him.

"Xavier! How are you? I'm sure you're a very happy man right now." Xavier grabbed Charles in a manly embrace patting him on the back in gratification over their latest coup.

"I'm ecstatic. I was worried for a moment there. Did you see how the stock dropped then recovered in the end? I was nervous as hell for a minute there." Xavier said his smile a mile wide across his face.

"I have to admit I was a little nervous too. That guy you saw me with? I talked him into a healthy investment that carried us to the end until I gave you the sign to sell. I don't think he left the men's room yet. When the stock bottomed out he said he thought he was going to be sick. He didn't even give me a chance to give him my spiel on the uncertainties of buying and selling. I got the feeling he's not too familiar with taking a loss." Charles smiled and put his arm around Xavier's shoulders and led him away from the noise and clean-up of the days' trading.

"Xavier, you know we have been working together for over a year now. You know?" Xavier cocked his head to the side and nodded yes wondering where the conversation was leading.

"You doubled your investment and you're now a very wealthy man. Wouldn't you agree?"

"Well, sorta. I'm cleaning up some bad investments I made so most of this money doesn't belong to me." Xavier said.

"That's too bad. But, that's not my problem. You still doubled your money. Remember when we met and I told you I could help out your investments periodically but you would have to return the favor one day? Well, it's time for you to pay." Charles continued not giving Xavier enough time to ask what it was he was expected to do in return.

"Go get yourself a room, have dinner and get some rest. I need you to meet me at my office around lunch time."

"Charles. I've never gone back on a deal but can this wait about a week? I gotta get back to the island and tie up some loose ends and then I am pretty much at your mercy."

"Tsk Tsk. Xavier, what's the rush? You're on the verge of resigning and your lease is up on that storefront you call an office. You're not trying to run away from your obligations are you?" Xavier immediately felt fear come over him. *How does Charles know so much about mt personal life?*

"Calm down Xavier. You got stiff all of a sudden. You'll be fine as long as you follow directions. You didn't think I wouldn't keep up with my protégé and investment did you? The dividends you've accrued from sound investments over the last six months should've afforded you that luxury. You made a lot of money from the information given to you. Now it's time to reciprocate in part. Now, loosen your tie, get a room and have drinks and dinner on me. I'll see you tomorrow."

What did I get myself into? I was just trying to start a business without being a slave to someone else. What was so wrong with that? His statement about my needing to disappear scares the hell out of me. I've just gotta calm down. No need to jump the gun. It can't be too serious. Charles knows I have just as much information on him as he has on me. Shit, I hold as many cards as he does.

**"Chandelle you've been quiet all day. This isn't like you. I'm nervous about what we're about to do and you who always calls the shots, hasn't said a mumbling word. What's up with you?"

"I'm okay sweetie. You were handling it today. I didn't need to say anything. I've just been planning ahead that's all."

"What do you mean planning ahead? Once we get my cousin, I'm *planning* that we get on the first plane outta here. I'm ready for some fun and sun girl. Nothing's wrong is it? I'm tired of all this ghetto drama."

"I don't know. We gotta worry about it later. Let's just handle this now and worry about other things later. We're here. I see your friend waving at the end of the alley. Drive down and pull over in front of him. Just make sure we have a clear path out of here." Rena crept down the back of the warehouse driving three miles an hour not to be heard by Slim and his boys inside. It was pitch black but she noticed that Smid's boys were positioning themselves outside their cars ready. Smid walked over to Rena's car and tapped on the drivers side window to get her attention.

"Rena, pull over and get out. Black and his boys are going to go in first. Chance, the tall one in front of the blue Camaro will come out and let us know when it's time for us to go in. Place the bag of money to pay the boys in the back seat of my car. That way I can pay them later. Remember that if something doesn't go as planned we'll meet back at the restaurant in the morning. You cool wit everything?" Rena nodded that she understood pulled the car in a position for a clean getaway and grabbed the gym bag to place in the back seat of Smid's car. Chandelle watched as her friend closed the back door of the dark blue vintage Monte Carlo then rushed to her side to whisper in her ear.

"Rena stay by me. I don't want you going inside and getting all emotional. We're gonna get your cousin then get the hell outta here."

"I'm cool Chandelle. Do you want me to hold the bag of money?" Chandelle gave a strong grip on the overnight bag. She planned on doing the right thing and paying the ransom but after not hearing from Xavier, she planned on holding on to every dime in the bag for a rainy day.

To hell with Slim. I worked too hard to get this money. I gotta feeling I'm gonna need this just to get back what is owed to me. I refuse to be stranded in Pittsburgh where I started with nothing!"

"Chandelle? Did you hear me? Stop day-dreamin' ho. Give me the bag. I'll pay him so we can get outta there fast."

"No Rena. I got it. You talk to that clown and I'll watch your back. You don't need to be trying to do everything. That's how mistakes happen." *I'm sorry Rena for not being up front. Just trust me girl.*

"Okay, Chandelle. Look! There goes the delivery guy. He's giving Smid the signal. They're about to go in!"

■■

Xavier waited by the elevator to reach Charles's office. The doorman alerted Charles that he arrived so he expected to be ushered into his office upon arrival. Charles always loved keeping him waiting. Xavier ignored his grand standing when they met on previous occasions. All the money Charles brought him made it easy to ignore the attention Charles demanded for his favors. But Xavier new this time was different and his palms began to sweat at the thoughts of what Charles had in store for him. Xavier entered the elevator and watched the lights above blink off the numbered floors being passed as he waited for the doors to open at the twentieth floor. The doors opened and as predicted, Charles was waiting on the other side to greet him.

"Xavier my man. Right on time! Walk with me to my office. Trust me this meeting isn't going to take long and I have another appointment in an hour." Xavier followed Charles to his office and took a seat across from his desk anxious to get the meeting over with.

"Xavier, can I offer you something to drink?" Charles pulled back a book from his book shelf that opened a panel and revealed a fully stocked bar behind it.

"No. It's a little early for me. Thank you." Xavier watched as Charles poured a drink in a rock glass over ice and moved towards his desk to be seated.

"It's never too early for a stiff one before business but enough of the pleasantries. In front of you is a manila envelope. I need you to deliver that envelope up town in two hours. Next to the manila envelope are the directions to who you should see and where you are going." Xavier exhaled a half sigh of relief but then the nervousness in his gut churned as it did earlier that morning.

"That's it? This seems a little too easy Charles. Anybody can deliver a package. Why me? How dangerous is this going to be?" Charles chuckled and took a sip of his drink and leaned back in his chair.

"Yes, that's it Xavier. It's as easy as that. But let me warn you. What you are holding is serious business and contains information that could change the lives of a lot of people involved. So, needless to say it's very valuable to its owner. You are to make sure you are on time and that the seal on that envelope isn't broken. It will be scanned under an infrared light to ensure the seal wasn't tampered with. I don't think I need to say what will happen to you if the envelope has been opened or lost. Don't ask any questions and follow any directions given to you. Once I receive a call that the package was delivered safely, you can consider your debt to me paid in full." Xavier shifted in his chair understanding the potential danger and wondered if he wanted to ask any questions and believed the less he knew the better off he would be.

"I just have one question man. You said that there was something inside this envelope that could make or break some people. Am I carrying drugs? I don't want to get involved in anything that has to do with drugs man. I get caught…"

Charles's laugh became louder and he almost choked onhis drink.

"It's not drugs Xavier. But I can't see you being worried about some drugs and what you've been involved in for the last year would put you in jail for life. If it were drugs in that small envelope you'd at least be able to see daylight again. That's the least of your problems. Just deliver the package. If everything works out maybe we can do some more business in the future." Xavier ignored his last comment not wanting to ask what was meant by the; if everything works out statement. *I got two hours to get this done then I'm on a plane outta here. This asshole never has to worry bout seeing me again.*

Chapter 14

Rena and Chandelle watched as Smid walked towardsall the while looking over his shoulder to make sure he wasn't being followed. Rena hesitated in walking towards him in sudden fear of what she would find out about what happened inside. Only ten minutes had passed since Black and his crew had gone inside to secure the warehouse.

"Let's go Rena. Let's get in and out. Black has the warehouse on lock down. " Smid said.

"I didn't hear any gunshots. Did everything go as planned? Is Nico okay?"

"Nico's cool. We had to smoke one of them. But only Slim and one of his soldiers are in there. I was told there were four of them. Either my sources were wrong which I doubt or his soldier are back any minute. We gotta get outta here without any surprises." Rena and Chandelle followed Smid closely and walked behind him through the door of the warehouse. Rena tried to focus her vision in the dark warehouse to locate Slim's location. There was a small glowing light in the middle of the floor from a small television set where she was able to see her cousin Nico tied to a chair with his head bowed down towards the table. He obviously wasn't coherent and looked as if he has been beaten badly over the last couple of days. Standing next to him was the man Rena recognized being with Slim the day she was approached in the garage of her apartment complex. Next to him Chance was standing with a gun pointing to his head.

"I wasn't expecting all this Rena. I underestimated you." Rena followed the voice and noticed Slim about five feet away from the table standing in the shadow with the young buck sticking a gun in his left side.

"Let my cousin go Slim. I'm here to pay you your money."

"You're in charge baby. Have your boy untie your cousin and leave the bag on the table. This can be squashed right here and now." Rena looked behind her towards Smid who then directed his soldier to untie Nico from the chair. Rena watched then asked for her cousin to be taken outside to safety. Once Nico was untied and heading towards the door, Rena asked Chandelle to place the bag on the table.

"There's your money Slim. We're done." Rena said.

"Let's go and get the hell outta here Rena." Chandelle whispered then began walking towards the door tugging at Rena's jacket to follow. Suddenly, a tussle was heard as Rome, who was left unguarded when Nico was taken outside, ran towards Black tackling him to the ground as they fought in the dark for the gun that was dropped. A swish was heard from the guns silencer and Rome was seen emerging from the dark quickly following behind Slim. Slim ran to the table for the bag and opened it for evidence that the money was inside. Chandelle pushed Rena towards the door hurrying her outside to get to the car. Everything seemed to be moving in slow motion as Chandelle fought to get to reach the car.

"Get that bitch Rome! The bag is empty! There's no money inside! Kill both dem bitches!" Rena froze for an instant wondering what the hell Slim was talking about. Chandelle nearly knocked her over fighting to get to the car in fear of being caught or shot. Chandelle noticed Rena's hesitation and ran slightly passed her and grabbed her arm to pull her to the alley.

"Run Rena! They're right behind us!" Chandelle watched as Smid loaded Nico in his car and he and his hired thugs were already driving out the alley.

Damn! These mother fuckers are the ones with the guns. They could've at least watched our back till we got to our car. We can't run to the car cause it's parked in the wrong direction towards the dead end. Its faced outward but we would have to drive past Slim and they could kill us before we make it out to the street. We gotta make a run for it out of the alley. Beckers Bar is on the front street and there's a party or something with all those people out front.

"Chandelle! I can't run that fast. They're gonna catch me!" Rena said trying to catch up with Chandelle after heading in the wrong direction towards the car. Chandelle looked over her shoulder and saw Rena struggling to keep up. Rome was gaining fast almost in arms reach of grabbing Rena.

"Rena! Get down! They're right behind you! C'mon heifer! Run!!", Rome grabbed Rena by the collar and dragged her to the ground. Chandelle was a few feet from the crowd and Slim gave up on the chase deciding that Rena's friend would suffice.

"Go 'head and run baby but you'll be back to get your girl or she's dead. Bring my shit and ya'll might live. Grab that bitch up Rome and throw her ass in the truck. Let's get the fuck out of here before anyone sees us." Chandelle ran towards the crowd and wept as Rena was being dragged by the collar towards the other end of the alley. She ducked behind a parked Escalade and watched Rena struggle to get loose. Rena screamed startling Rome who briefly loosened his grip allowing her to grab the gun Rome had tucked in the waist of his pants. Rena fired twice hitting Rome in the chest and stomach. Rome writhed in pain before hitting the ground. Slim turned hearing Rome's scream and saw Rena now pointing a gun in his direction.

"Whatcha gonna do with that gun beautiful? You don't want to do this." Slim said holding up both his hands in the air but not moving a muscle.

"I'm gonna kill you, you asshole. I told you I didn't have your money and I don't fuck with drugs but you wouldn't listen. You couldn't take what I gave you in the first place and leave me and my family alone. You had to get greedy. Now I'm taking you outta here and I won't have to worry bout your ass no more."

"Okay okay my bad. I thought you were bullshittin' but hey I gotcha. Let's just call it squashed. I'll forget about it. Cool?" Slim said begging for his life.

"Too late for that now you bastard."

What's going on down there? I called the police! They're on their way! Rena heard the voice moving towards her and scanned the alley for a way to get out without being noticed. Sirens were in the distance and she knew she didn't have a lot of time. Rena pulled the trigger and watched as Slim hit the ground. She wasn't sure if he was dead but knew she'd hit her target even with the distance and in the darkness darkness. Satisfied she tucked the gun in the small of her back and headed to the far end of the alley.

Chapter 15

Xavier stood outside the Embassy on Wall Street and opened the envelope that detailed the directions for his package delivery.

Take the A train to Harlem. Once you leave the subway, make a left onto 125th street past the Apollo Theatre to 125th and Adam Creighton Powell Blvd. On the corner to your right you will see the Harlem State Office Building. Go inside to the fifteenth floor where you will be greeted by a guard. Show the guard the pass enclosed in the envelope and he will buzz you inside. Once you get inside, knock on the third door on your right. Show the secretary the envelope and you will then be given further instructions. Be sure to follow these directions without any deviations and arrive promptly by noon. If you are late or the contents of the manila envelope are damaged, it could be costly. Xavier checked his watch and saw that it was ten. He figured it would take him about an hour to get to his destination. *The note didn't say anything about my being early.*

I'm going to head over there now and hope I can get this over with early and reach the airport before rush hour traffic. I'll stay at the airport on standby. I just pray that I'm not over my head with this. Xavier headed to the nearest subway station. Xavier boarded and held on as the train whizzed through past the stops. His past experiences taught him not to engage in any needless conversations. New York was not the kind of place out- of- towners took lightly. Only three months earlier two young thugs attempted to set him up by asking for change to distract him while the other tried to snatch his briefcase and jump out the train at the approaching stop. It was an old con but Xavier figured his demeanor was a dead giveaway to him being from out of town. He was able to hold on to his briefcase because he was stronger than the thug who attempted to rob him as the young boy fell to the concrete when his shirt got caught in the door. But what really amazed him was that no one on the train came to his aid. Xavier knew then to just stare out the window and stay cool so that no one would pay him enough attention to try him again. Xavier soon became cognizant of what it meant to have a New York state of mind and saw nothing becoming oblivious to anything and everyone around him.Moments later, the subway stopped and Xavier stepped off the train and headed toward the steps towards 125th street. He followed the directions heading down 125th and walked towards the Harlem State Office Building where he entered and walked to the elevators rode to the fifteenth floor. He flashed the badge at the guard and waited for the door to buzz. It took only five steps to reach the third door on the right. Xavier paused to read the name on the door. *Gainer and Associates. Hmmm, so far so good. Here we go.* Xavier said to himself. He knocked on the door and opened it to a light skinned young lady in her early thirties at the receptionist desk.

"Can I help you sir?" Xavier retrieved the envelope from his inside left jacket pocket and handed it to the secretary.

"I'm Xavier Barnes and I'm simply here to drop this off."

"Please have a seat. Someone will be with you in a moment." The secretary gave a weak smile and disappeared behind a door on the right side of her desk. Two minutes later a short stalky man in his late fifties appeared and ushered him inside. Xavier took a seat offered by the gentleman as he watched him pick up the receiver of his phone and punch in a couple of numbers on the keypad.

"The courier is here." Xavier heard him say. The gentleman then listened to what was being said on the other line then hung up the phone.

"You're a little early but we can accommodate you. I'm glad to see you were able to make it." Xavier wasn't sure if he should respond or wait to see what all of this was about. Before he could say anything the door opened to three men entering. One stood on each side of Xavier and the third stood by the behind the desk with a box that resembled a time clock without a face. He picked up the envelope from the desk and turned flipped a switch on the box that emanated a red light and waved the envelope under the light.

"It's clean Mr. Gainer." Xavier watched as he handed the envelope to the man who ushered him in the office. Mr. Gainer opened the envelope and read the contents of the letter inside.

He then turned the envelope over and held the key that fell out onto the desk.

"What the fuck is this?" Mr. Gainer's neck became beet red that traveled to his face. The two men on each side of Xavier moved in closer towards his chair as if to grab him if he were to try to run.

"Mr. Gainer, I don't know what you are talking about. I was just told to deliver the envelope. I don't know anything about what it contains." Xavier said becoming nervous.

"You know exactly what I'm talking about. You're a part of these crooks and their schemes. I paid good money for the information I was supposed to receive. This is more of your games! I warned your buddies that if I didn't get what I paid for, somebody was going to pay." Xavier searched the room looking for a way out. He even contemplated screaming if it was going to get him out alive.

"I swear I didn't do anything. Please sir, let me make a phone call. I believe I can clear this up for you. Charles told me…"

before Xavier could finish his statement the two goons on each side of him snatched him from the chair and began punching him in the face and stomach.

"Take him outta here down the back stairwell. We'll show him and his cronies they can't fuck with us." Xavier struggled to get loose from the grip of the men who were now using him as a punching bag.

"Wait! Wait! Maybe I can pay you for your loss! Please hear me out!"

"Put him in the chair. Let me hear what he has to say. You better make this worth my while. I have an appointment."

"I have money in the bank. I can wire it to any account of your choice. Tell me how much."

"It's gonna cost you a million dollars." Xavier's chest sank when he heard the amount. It was just about all the money he had. He knew the million would put back in the hole owing his friend and throwing away his dream of starting over.

"Okay. I can have the money wired to you by tomorrow." Gainer began to laugh as if his suggestion was outrageous.

"Son, you can't be serious. You can't believe that I'm going to allow you to walk out of here and trust that you will send me a wire transfer to my account. I wouldn't allow you to have access to my account to trace the funds. I want one million dollars on my desk in cash in an hour." Fear rose across Xavier's face searching for a way to come up with a million in cash in a hour.

"You look sick. You either have the money or you don't." Mr. Gainer said instructing with his finger to carry Xavier out of his office.

"I have the money. I just gotta figure out where I can cash the funds out in cash."

"If that's the problem you came to the right place. Harlem National Bank is two blocks from here. It's a black owned bank who I'm sure would be happy to help out a brotha." Gainer said laughing at his use of the word brotha. "They deal

206

with these types of transactions for a small fee. I'll have my men here escort you to the bank while you get the money. If you try anything funny, you won't make it out alive. Do you understand me? You can work out the fees at the bank. If it's true you don't have anything to do with my being taken, you can go back to your sources to get your money back."

"I swear I won't try anything funny. But I do have a couple of questions. How do I know that you'll let me go when you get the money? Secondly, how can you trust that after I pay you I won't call the police?" Xavier wasn't sure if he wanted to ask the second question but figured that if he answered, he had an idea whether he needed a plan of escape because Gainer didn't have intentions on letting him live.

"You got balls son." Gainer sat at his desk and fished for a cigar from the humidor located in his top drawer. He lit the cigar and blew out three perfect circles of smoke before he continued, "I'm gonna let you go cause I kinda believe that you got mixed up in something over your head. You were too calm when you came in here. You obviously don't have a clue to what I was expecting in the envelope. To answer your second question, it would be stupid to contact the police. If you use my name in any connection with our transaction you will not only risk your life but the lives of all the people involved who sent you here. Again, you don't have a clue to what you're involved in. Your ignorance might just have save your life. Now, go get my money." Xavier rose from the chair and fixed his suit jacket and walked to the door along with his escorts.

Chapter 16

Rena ran through the bushes to avoid the police who were on their way. She stopped periodically to view the alley for anybody who might spot her as she tried to make her way to the street. *I hear the sirens. Please Lord let me make it out of here. I only have a little way to go to make to the street.* Rena saw the man moving closer up the alley trying to view the bodies that were lying in the street. She saw her chance to sneak out the bushes and blend in with the crowd who were drinking and bringing the party outside the bar. Rena ran to the middle of the street to the sidewalk where a woman who was leaving the party was walking towards her car.

"Excuse me. Can I bother you for a ride? I just need to get to a phone." The woman looked her up and down and hesitated when she saw the condition of Rena's hair and clothes.

"I don't think I'm going in your direction."

"Please. My car broke down and I was trying to fix it myself. I just need to call my friend to pick me up." The woman hesitated then used her remote to open the doors to her vehicle.

"Thank you so much. I have some money to pay you." Rena dug in her pocket and offered the woman a twenty. After seeing the money, the woman became more relaxed that she wasn't going to be robbed and offered Rena the use of her phone. Rena quickly thanked her and called Chandelle's cell phone in hopes that she would answer and didn't leave the phone in her car. Three rings later Chandelle answered.

"Chandelle, it's me."

"Rena! Oh my Goodness Rena! I was so scared that I wouldn't hear from you again! Where are you? Are you okay?" Chandelle said screaming into the phone.

"I'm fine. Listen, I caught a ride and I'm on my way to the Eat N' Park. Can you meet me there?"

"Yes. I'm walking through the plaza parking lot. I'll meet you there in five minutes." Rena hung up the phone and directed the woman to the Eat N' Park to meet Chandelle.

■■■

Chandelle stood outside the restaurant waiting for Rena to pull up. Rena exited the car and ran into the arms of her best friend.

"Rena, I'm so glad you're alive! Girl, I walked almost all the way here from the bottoms and cried the entire way."

"You're glad? I'm still in shock! Let's get out of here. I don't want to go inside and I don't want to be down here in the Rocks for another minute. Call us a cab." Chandelle took the phone from her pants pocket and called a cab. She informed the dispatcher that they were headed to the airport.

"Chandelle, we can't go to the airport now. I don't have any money, a change of clothes or my passport."

"Don't worry about it. I have your passport and money in a bag in a locker at the airport. Remember when I told you I had to get the money to pay Slim? I decided then that I wasn't going to give him shit. You already gave him money. He'd blackmail you forever. Besides, I haven't heard from Xavier."

"I'm going to jump on you about not giving Slim the money and not telling me later. But what does Xavier have to do with this? You've been worried about him since you got here."

"I gave him our money to invest Rena." Rena raised her left eyebrow waiting to hear the rest of the story that didn't come.

"You told me before you left that you were going to invest some money with him. If he's making us money what's the big deal?"

"I gave him everything. Well everything except for the fifty thousand and a couple thousand more for travel money. I figured that if he doubled or tripled our money as planned we would be set for life. And by the time I got back we wouldn't be so hard pressed to open up a business to keep our money rolling in."

"What? So, are you telling me you haven't heard from him since you gave him the money?"

"Exactly. I fucked up. We gotta get to the islands to find our money."

"What makes you think he's still there? If he stole it, he's not going to be there for you to just walk up on him and say hello." Rena said sarcastically.

"He's not there. He's in New York. He had to meet his friend on Wall Street. I'm thinking that if we get to the islands I'm pretty sure I can get some information on his whereabouts."

"I hope so Chandelle. Do you realize we will be right back where we started? Even worse is that we'll be broke and can't move back to Pittsburgh with our friends and family for help."

"I know Rena. But we made it this far. We have a couple of dollars in our pockets and nothing to lose."

"Here comes the cab. Let's get out of here. Remind me to call my cousin tomorrow. I want to make sure he's okay. Oh, and when we get on the plane I have something else to tell you."

Chandelle looked at Rena challenging her to tell her now but changed her mind knowing that getting their money back was more important. Everything else could wait.

Chapter 17

"Walk in the bank nice and easy and ask to speak to the bank manager. Let him know exactly what you're trying to do and if you do anything stupid you'll never walk out of here alive." Gainer's goon showed Xavier the gun he had in a holster hidden in the inside of his suit jacket.

"Look to your left by the customer service desk. There's a small table with two chairs. We'll be sitting there with a clear view to the inside of the manager's office. Hank and I will be watching you." Xavier never said a word. He opened the door and headed straight to the bank manager's office for assistance.

"Excuse me. I need your assistance. I need to draw on an out of town account and withdrawal a sizable amount of money." The manager listened intently and placed his pen on his desk and rose from his desk to introduce himself.

"Please come in sir. My name is Miles Jacobs and I'm the branch manager here at Harlem National. I'll be happy to help you. What is your name?"

"My name is Xavier Barnes." Xavier took out his billfold that contained his passport, drivers' license and social security card and placed them on the desk.

"It's nice to meet you Mr. Barnes. What bank would you like to make the withdrawal from?"

" The Caribbean Bank and Trust in St. Croix, Virgin Islands. I have my routing number and checking account number." Xavier pulled his checkbook from his billfold to retrieve the check.

"Oh, I see. We can get a wire transfer for you and get a cashier check that you can cash at the teller window. How much would you like to transfer Mr. Barnes?"

"A million dollars." Mr. Jacobs froze, shocked at the amount and recovered seizing the opportunity to earn a bonus for landing a huge account.

"Mr. Barnes, we offer the best services you can probably ask for here at Harlem national. Allow me to introduce you to some of the benefits of opening…" Xavier interrupted his selling pitch before he could finish.

"I'm sure you offer great rates here but I'm not trying to open an account. I'm simply trying to do a wire transfer as expeditiously as possible. I'm going to need cash money." Mr. Jacobs cleared his throat at the request and silently asked if there were any problems he should be made aware of. He continued to explain that the bank offered discreet services for times such as these.

"I assure you Mr. Jacobs that I'm aware of what I'm doing. I need the cash to handle a business transaction here in New York."

"Okay, Mr. Barnes. Before I can complete the transaction, I will have to get the approval of either the Vice President or President of the bank. Their offices are located on the top floor. I am not authorized to approve such a large request. Please be patient till I come back. Can I get you something to drink while you wait?"

"No. I'm fine thank you." Mr. Jacobs stood from his desk and headed to the elevator to the top floor of the bank. Xavier watched as the bank manager left the office then waited a minute to search the bank for the escorts that were hired to keep an eye on him. Xavier saw the one named Hank pretending to be reading the newspaper while the other one stared at him from across the room. Ten minutes had passed and the bank manager still hadn't returned with the bank officers. Xavier again turned to see his bodyguards and noticed Hank rise from the chair to walk towards the office where he was seated. Xavier watched him take three steps when his eyes followed two men who exited the elevator. He slowly turned and sat in his chair and peered over the newspaper he was reading.

"Mr. Barnes. I'm so sorry to keep you waiting. Xavier stood to shake the hand who he assumed was the hand of the bank president.

"My name is Alexander Wright. I am the CEO and part owner here at Harlem National Bank. My two brothers and I are the majority stockholders of the bank." Alexander smiled brightly. "Well, enough of the small talk. I understand that you'd like to withdrawal a million dollars from your bank account."

"Yes, I would. I gave all the information to your bank manager."

"I don't mean to be so bold Mr. Barnes but I'd like to ask you a couple of questions if I may. We don't get these types of requests every day. Such sizable withdrawals are usually made by businessmen who prearrange these withdrawals especially for tax purposes. No one wants to overpay the tax man. You know what I mean?" Mr. Wright began laughing lightly at his own joke.

"I'm sorry I didn't call ahead of time. I was assured that your bank wouldn't have any problems fulfilling my request."

"I assure you we don't. We just want to make sure all of the I's are dotted and all of the t's are crossed. If you can follow me up to my office Mr. Barnes we can handle your business. I'll be handling your transfer personally and I want to let you know up front that there will be some rather substantial fees that will have to be taken care of. I assume are prepared to handle the fees?" Xavier slowly turned around to eye the gentlemen who followed him into the bank. He wasn't sure what their reaction would be when they saw him being escorted onto the elevator and out of their sight. He thought about excusing himself to explain the situation to Hank and his friend but decided against it for fear that they may not believe him and would very well shoot him on the spot. He figured he'd take his chances and get on the elevator and they'd wait for his return. When he returned with the money it should calm their fears that everything went as planned.

"Yes, I'm sure I can handle the fees. Just show me to your office and we can get started." Xavier stood and sandwiched himself between the Mr. Jacobs and Mr. Wright as a safety shield just in case Gainer's men decided to open fire.

Chandelle leaned her head back against the headrest with her eyes closed in hopes of devising a plan once she landed in St. Croix.

We should land in St. Croix earlier enough to pay a visit to Xavier's office. He's not answering his phone and I'm sure he's not at work but this will give me an opportunity to have a heart to heart with his work companion Mike. There is something between them that I can't put my finger on. I know I can get something useful out of him. If I can't, I still have the address and phone number of his office. I can pay a visit there and see what I can find out around his office. The complex is nearly deserted and under development so I'm not worried about anyone taking any real interest in my being there.

"Chandelle, Are you awake?" Rena whispered loudly in Chandelle's ear.

"Back up girl! You're loud enough! Yes, I'm awake." Chandelle said sitting up straight in her chair.

"Remember I told you that I had something to tell you?"

"Yeah, I remember. What's up?"

"Girl, I killed Rome boy and I think I killed Slim too." Rena said trying not to cry.

"I kinda figured that Rena. I didn't want to bring it up or ask you any questions about how you got away cause I didn't want you to go into shock or have a nervous breakdown or something along those lines. Try not to think about it. We can get you some psychiatric treatment later." Chandelle said turning her head to look out the window.

"What?!" Rena said loud enough for the entire plane to hear her.

"Ssshh, Rena!"

"This is serious Chandelle. I have two maybe three bodies under my belt. I've become a trained hit man! A killer!"

"Calm down Rena. I know you're serious. I'm not making fun of the situation. I just don't want you trippin over it now. You're not a killer. Well, maybe you are. But you killed in self-defense. You didn't go out and kill on a contract or anything. You'll be fine. Nobody knows you did anything and no one knows where you are. Everything will be okay."

"I hope you're right. I don't want to be a killer but I hope Slim is dead. I couldn't wait around to make sure cause there was somebody coming up the alley and I didn't want him to see me."

"Slim is another drug dealer that nobody is going to give a fuck about. What is he going to tell the police? He was holding someone hostage in a warehouse he had no business in and they escaped and shot him? I don't think so. Besides, the streets will love to see him dead. Your contact isn't going to tell because he would be implicated in a crime. There are too many niggas on the come up working for him that would love to take his position in the streets."

"You're right. I'm so glad you're back. I mean you have been here with me but not really. You hardly said anything for the last two days. Now you're back reassuring me and taking over. I feel so much better."

"Im okay Rena. I've always been here with you. You had it worked out on your end. Now I gotta fix things on mine. Once we clear up this last problem, we'll be home free."

Chapter 18

Xavier surveyed the plush, dimly lit office in awe as to how close he was to having a future similar to the one Alexander was enjoying. Xavier desired his own successful business, a beautiful office with a view and a building full of employees working for him. Now it was all gone because of a greedy mistake he made a few short months ago. Alexander Wright spread Xavier's documents across his desk and turned his computer on and waited for it to power up before beginning begin the process of the wire transfer. Alexander looked up from his computer and spoke to Xavier.

"Mr. Barnes, I couldn't help but to notice how nervous you looked leaving my branch manager's office. I also noticed that you repeatedly turned your head towards the door as if you were being watched or if you were looking for someone."

"What if I told you that I was in trouble? Would it make a difference? I'm just talking hypothetically here of course."

Xavier said hoping there could be a happy ending to his nightmare.

"Well, hypothetically of course, I'd ask you to tell you to explain the problem at hand and then I would possibly give you a solution on how to fix your problem." Xavier pondered his reply and wondered what he had to lose.

"How much would these services cost someone who was interested in your proposition?"

"It depends on the services needed and rendered. Let me just say it wouldn't cost nearly as much you are trying to spend now."

"Look, Mr. Wright, I would love to lay my cards out on the table but I don't want to find myself in deeper than I already am."

"I understand Xavier. I can call you Xavier can't I? Xavier nodded yes.

"How about if I ask you a couple of questions so that you won't compromise your position. Then I will be able to tell by your answers if I would be able to help you. Deal?"

"Deal."

"Did you kill someone?"

"No."

"Good. Are you involved or have you made a deal with the Mafia?" Xavier hesitated not sure how to answer.

"Not that I know of. I don't know who I'm involved with."

"Hmm. I'm going to assume for a moment that it's not the mob. You have been in my office now for at least a half an hour and my bank hasn't been shot up because they are downstairs looking for you. As far as I can tell, no one is outside casing the place."

"How would you know?" Xavier asked.

"I have resources. Let me say that a Black man who owns the largest bank in Harlem can't be too careful. I have enemies of my own simply because of my good fortune." Xavier shook his head satisfied with his answer.

"Do you know anybody that is involved in what brought you here?"

"Yes. But only briefly."

"Okay, Xavier that's good. I like to have an idea of some of the players involved.

"You're from the islands. Is that correct?"

"Yes. I guess my accent is a clean give away." Xavier stated trying to make light of a serious situation.

"I think I may be able to help you. But first you're going to have to explain the entire story without leaving out anything. If you leave out anything, I can't be responsible for what can happen if something goes wrong." Mr. Wright said leaning back in his chair ready to devise a plan for his clients' freedom.

"There really isn't anything for me to tell. I have been working with a colleague of mine on Wall Street. For the past year he has been giving me some insider information on the stock market. I have been using this information for my own personal gain and for some clients of mine to help build my own brokerage firm. In exchange for the information he told me that one day I would be called on to take care of a favor at his request. Well, yesterday my number came up. He asked that I deliver a package to Gainer and Associates at the Harlem State Office Building. I met with Mr. Gainer who opened the package that contained a letter and a key. Once he read the letter he went off saying that he didn't get what he paid for and somebody had to pay for his loss. That somebody was me. He agreed that if I paid him a million dollars he would let me live. That's how I arrived here." Alexander shook his head back and forth and sat straight up in his chair.

"What's wrong Mr. Wright? Is there anything you can possibly do to help me?" Xavier queried , the desperation apparent in the beads of perspiration now gathering on the bridge of his nose.

"Yes, I can help you. Today seems to be your lucky day."

" I'm relieved and thankful you can help me but how can you be so sure?"

"Like I said before, I'm well known in New York and I have a lot of business interests here. Sometimes there are things going on here that I make my business. I know all about your friend Charles and Mr. Gainer. You've been set up. They are part of a sting operation that they run time and time again to get to hungry naïve guys like yourself looking for some fast money. Charles sets you up to make some money on some insider stocks. He throws you some valuable information from time to time with you trusting his information. Then he urges you to make a large investment on some bad information. He convinces you that he will make good the next time and then gives you an opportunity to make a huge score. That's when he cashes in on his favor. He sets you up with his partner, Mr. Gainer. Gainer blames you for a deal gone bad and extorts the money you just scored from the market back to him and Charles. It's easy untraceable money." Xavier jumps from his chair in anger not realizing he was being played for a fool all along.

"I'm gonna kill him! That asshole had me thinking that I was about to die on some bullshit plan that he rigged up with a partner! I'm gonna kill him!"

"Slow down Xavier. You still have a problem. I'm sure you could probably take Charles on and do some serious damage but he is heavily connected. Those two fools didn't come up with this plan on their own. They pay off quite a few people to pull this off. I have at least two to three marks a month on this scam. You are talking a lot of money. They couldn't do something this major alone." Xavier sat back down in his chair again worried when he realized what Mr. Wright said made sense.

"What do I do now?"

"We are going to have to get you out of here. I can have security escort you out of the bank through the back entrance. You will be taken in one of my cars to a safe place till we can get you a new identification and start somewhere no one knows you."

"Safe place? You mean this won't be over today? I don't want to stay in New York any longer than I have to."

"I understand. It will take a day or two to get you a clean passport. We'll try to make arrangements for your new start in a place of your choosing. How does that sound?"

"I guess I don't have a choice. How much is this going to set me back?"

"Somewhere around two hundred and fifty grand." Xavier nearly went into shock after hearing the cost.

"Two hundred and fifty grand? Can't you get me something a little better than that figure? I have to start my life all over."

"That is a generous offer Xavier. You were about to pay a million and go home to start your life all over. The passport is a rush job. If you're willing to stay longer, I may be able to knock a few thousand off the top. I like you Xavier. It could have been more."

"No. I'm not willing to stay any longer than a couple of days. I'll take the deal."

I'll be happy if not another person in my life tells me that they like me. Every time I hear it, it costs me money.

"Okay. Let's get that money from your account then we can get you out of here. I'm sure you are ready to relax, have a good meal and make plans for where you would like to go.

Chapter 19

"Where are we going Chandelle?" Rena looked out the window of the cab taking in the scenic island of St. Croix. She knew her visit here was going to be cut short and the plan for her and Chandelle to make it their home was all but null and void.

"We're going to Morton and Meyers Brokerage firm. Xavier took me there to see where he worked and show me how the stock market worked. He had a friend that he introduced me to that worked with him named Mike."

"You think Mike is going to give up his boy? What the hell have you been smoking? That's a long shot."

"I don't think their relationship was all that. They worked together but their seemed to be some kind of competition thing going on between them or something. Plus the way he was checking me out, I now he was kinda interested. Maybe I can use that to get him to talk to me."

"Girl, you going to make sure you get yourself attention ain't you?"

"Wasn't even like that. There wasn't anything going on between Xavier and me and Mike tested the waters. Xavier told him that I was interested in doing some business with him. Mike's reaction is what really caught my attention. I later heard him telling Xavier that he was warned by the boss about creating investment portfolios with friends or lovers. His boss said it was bad for business and that if they brought somebody they knew to the firm who was interested in investing, they were supposed to pass them off to someone else and they would receive a bonus for the referral. Mike thought things were a little shady I think."

"So, you think Mike can tell us where Xavier is or give us some information on where to find him?"

"I hope so. It's a start. I have another lead I want to check out if that one is cold."

"We're here. Just follow my lead. Don't say anything and don't go into here with an attitude."

"I know how to keep my mouth closed. I'll be as charming as I can be." Chandelle and Rena entered the building taking the elevator to the twentieth floor. The elevator doors opened and Chandelle and Rena were greeted by a receptionist who wasn't at her desk during her first visit with Xavier.

"Hi, may I help you?" The receptionist said in her best customer service voice.

"Yes, I'm here to see Mike. Is he here?" The receptionist eyed Chandelle up and down and hesitated to call Mike because Chandelle wasn't dressed as a client and didn't want to repeat a past mistake of allowing a disgruntled client onto the floor wreaking havoc.

"Do you have an appointment? What is your name?"

"My name is Chandelle Carter. I had recently met with Mike. If you call him I'm sure he will see me." The receptionist picked up the phone to call Mike when Chandelle saw him walking towards his cubicle to answer his phone. She frantically began to wave to get his attention just in case he may have forgotten who she was and denied her request for a visit. Mike paused briefly, then smiled recognizing her familiar face. The receptionist hung up the phone to apologize to Chandelle that he didn't answer the phone when Mike interrupted her apology.

"Thanks Cindy. I'll handle this. Chandelle right?"

"Yes. Hi, Mike. How are you? Do you have a few minutes?" Mike smiled genuinely and escorted Chandelle and Rena to a small private staff lounge to talk. Rena made herself useful watching Ellen on the television so Chandelle could have his full attention.

"What can I do for you Chandelle?"

"I need your help Mike. Remember the last time I was here with Xavier? I overheard you tell Xavier that he should follow the rules about creating a portfolio for me because we were friends. Remember"

"I didn't know you heard that but yes I remember. Our company has rules about investing for friends and family. Why do you ask?"

"Well, I allowed Xavier to invest some money for me and I haven't heard from him since and that was over a week ago. I need to find him and I was hoping that you could help me."

"Wow Chandelle." Mike ran his hands through his hair contemplating what to do. He didn't want to get Xavier into any trouble but Xavier no longer worked for the company and really didn't think he had anything to tell her that could possibly hurt him.

"I haven't heard from Xavier in a couple days either Chandelle. He called the day after I met you and asked that I leave a message with the boss that he was taking a few days off. He told me that he was going to New York. I later heard that he no longer worked for the company."

"Hmmm. I knew he was going to New York. In fact, he said he was going straight to Wall Street to conduct some business on my behalf."

"He visits New York quite often. He and I were cool and I knew he was trying to someday open his own firm so it wasn't odd he would be visiting but it blew my mind that he no longer worked here. I don't know all the information about why though. I just figured that the fact we were friends he would call me when he got settled and fill me in." Chandelle was getting that Mike didn't know any more than she already did. Feeling desperate she reached for his hand hoping that the sexy eyes he was giving her was a play at letting her know he was interested in her. She saw it as a chance to dig deep and find out anything that he may not think is important.

"He told me that he had a friend there he was working with. I hate to say this because I know he was your friend and I don't know a lot about how the market works but I'm worried about him." Chandelle said trying to turn her concerns around to seem sympathetic toward Xavier.

"What do you mean you're worried about him?"

"Well he was telling me about a friend of his that helped him out from time to time on Wall Street. Anyway, he said that his friend would give him information on stocks to buy that could bring in a good deal of money. I asked him if it was illegal or what they called insider trading. He said sort of but brokers did it all the time."

"Are you serious? Chandelle if what you are saying is true, you're right. That is illegal. If you get caught with information about how stocks are going to go up or down you can do a lot of jail time. So, don't tell me, you gave him money to invest right? Mike said shaking his head.

"Yes, I did. But I'm not worried about the money as much as I'm worried about Xavier's safety. *I'm not lying about that one. When I catch his ass, I'm going to kill him.* Xavier said something about this being his last trade with this person because it was becoming dangerous. Do you remember him ever giving you a name or address of anybody he was staying with? I need to talk to him. I just need to know that he's okay." Chandelle said lying.

"Damn! I'm wondering what my boy got himself into. Let me think. I remembering him once that he said he was having lunch with a fellow broker named Charles. I can't remember his last name. I just know that he is always on the exchange floor. He said that dude stayed on the floor watching the numbers daily like he owned every piece of stock for every company on the tape. I don't really know anything else. I guess you can find him if the dude is there on the regular. What are you going to do Chandelle?"

"I don't know. I might go to New York if I don't hear from him. I don't know."

I'm gonna check out his office for more clues then my ass is on the first thing smoking out of here straight to the N-Y-C.

"Well, I know you're concerned about Xavier but if you're planning to stay in town for a few days I'd love to take you out to dinner." *Oh boy, here we go.* Chandelle thought to herself. Putting on her best smile as to being flattered she said,

"Mike, I'd love to take you up on your offer but I can't. I don't know if you noticed but I'm here with my friend who I'm showing around town. We have to leave tomorrow so she can get back to work. We're thinking about moving here so I hope the offer stands."

"Absolutely. Let me get you my card so you can call me when you get in." *Not in this lifetime.* Chandelle thanked Mike for his time and reassured him that he would be hearing from her, shook his hand and left. Chandelle and Rena boarded the elevator on their way to Xavier's office to see if they could find out any more information that would help her find him in New York.

∎∎∎

Xavier sat in the back of the Cadillac Escalade headed to Queens to a safe-house where he would be staying until his passport arrived for him to leave the country.

I can't believe this shit I'm in. I withdrew every penny I had to get out of this mess and start a new life. I'm gonna miss Brian though. We had some good times together. Good friends are hard to find. I know by this time Chandelle is wondering where I am. I kinda feel bad about the fucked up situation I'm leaving her in. I kinda like the sista and she was fine as hell. I gotta let that shit go though. I didn't have any plans on ever seeing her again anyway. I think I'm headed to Barbados. I can't get away from my island roots. I know I'll be safe there for at least a little while. Damn! My money's fucked up! Charles called himself helping me out and the whole time he was taking me for a goddamn joy ride! I gotta think how I'm gonna continue to live comfortably and still keep a hefty bank account. I guess I can start a business in Barbabos but if I get lucky and make some money it may draw too much attention to me. Xavier tried to think about anything about money. He began to just stare at the passing houses and notice how poorer people were living the farther away they were from the city.

Oh hell no! I can't live like this! Let me think. I got two million dollars which ain't shit if you think about it. I took a million from Chandelle and I broke even on the scheme dealing with Charles. I was hoping to use that million to start over and give the other million to Brian clean up my debt with him. I would've had less money than I do now but I would be starting over with the clients I already have. I wouldn't buy any clothes and I wouldn't be running from anybody but Chandelle, who wouldn't find me anyway cause she doesn't know my clients. Now I have to pay the Wright brothers a quarter of a mil to get me out of town, find a place to live. I can't call my clients and get their money cause that would only set off red flags to people who know me on how to find me. This shit is just like being broke. I gotta start all over. I can't even call my boy cause I owe him money. Fuck it. I got about a mil and a half after expenses that'll have to do. I just can't live like I'm used to living. I'm going to have to lay low for a while and slum it. Shit, there are people worse off than I am. I'm just not that brother used to being worse off.

The driver lowered the divider between him and Xavier to alert him that they had arrived. Xavier quickly went into shock noticing that the apartment where he was going to have to spend the next day or two was nothing more than a dilapidated building where most of the windows had been covered with boards and the outside walls were covered in graffiti naming Buster as the artist.

"Are you serious? Man this place doesn't look safe." The driver opened the drivers' side door and laughed as he headed towards the hatch of the SUV to retrieve some belongings to help make his stay a little more comfortable. Xavier watched as he checked out the driver button his jacket upon leaving the vehicle but not before he saw the gun hidden inside his waistband. The gun made Xavier nervous but figured in this neighborhood it was better to be safe than sorry. He also knew Mr. Wright was an important man and probably had enemies that may have to be dealt with. Xavier suddenly felt more safe than concerned.

"It's cool man. That's why they call it a safe house. Nobody pays it any attention and it doesn't look worth robbing or loitering around. You'll see. I think you'll be quite surprised once your inside." Xavier watched silently as the driver lifted the hatch on the SUV and pulled his luggage onto the curb to take them inside the boarded row house.

"Follow me. I'll take you inside and show you where everything is." Xavier grabbed his carryon and followed up the steps behind the driver inside the house.

"Let's go upstairs first to your room and work our way back down towards the back of the house to the kitchen."

"This doesn't look too bad. In fact it's kinda nice. If it wasn't so dark in here, a brotha could get used to this place. By the way, what's your name?" Xavier asked as they headed down the hallway to the massive bedroom at the front of the house.

"My name is Raul. I told you this spot is comfortable. It is a little hidden secret for situations like yours. It's only used occasionally. Mr. Wright keeps it boarded up to cut down on costs of having someone here to take care of the place and make sure its not robbed or looted. As long as it looks empty the locals don't mess with it. Every once in a while we might see a board messed with by one of the junkies trying to get in to get out of the cold or trying to find a place to hide while they fix. It has a up to date ventilation system so that fresh air is circulated through the place."

"Very nice. I can see a man in his position putting something like this together. He's a smart man."

"Yeah. Mr. Wright says he's out to make money not to waste it." Raul set the bags down at the door and opened the door to the bathroom inside the master suite.

"This is your bedroom. There is a phone in here and behind that cabinet is a flat screen. The Knicks are on tonight if you're interested. There seems to be everything you need in the bathroom. Follow me. I'll take you downstairs to show you the rest of the house." Xavier set his bag on the bed and followed Raul down the steps.

"To your left is the living room and to your right is the dining room. The dining room leads into the kitchen in the back of the house." Xavier scanned the massive chef style kitchen and opened the refrigerator to fully stocked shelves and a six pack of beer on the bottom shelf.

"If you don't want to cook anything, I can leave you the number to a restaurant that will deliver something to you. Let them know the address and they will know what to do from there. They were hired to take care of all of Mr. Wrights' associates so they will be very discreet without asking any off the wall questions. They will ring a buzzer to the door in the back to let you know the food has arrived. You don't have to worry about the bill or the tip. It'll be handled later."

"Mr. Wright has taken care of everything hasn't he? I'm not very hungry right now. I think I'm just going to take a shower and grab a beer and take in the game as you suggested."

"Okay. If you need anything call the number by the phone upstairs in your room. Do you need anything else? I can suggest some good company if you'd like for me to arrange that for you." Xavier smiled at the suggestion and considered the offer for a quick second then realized he would be too wound up in his thoughts to perform.

"No. Thanks though. Maybe next time." Raul shook his head and told Xavier he would get a call the next day to give him an update from Mr. Wright. Xavier walked Raul to the door and secured the lock on the front door.

Chapter 20

Chandelle sat in the very chair that Xavier sat in days before showing her information related to his business and selling her on the idea that investing her money with him was going to make her a very rich and comfortable woman. She wished she would've slowed down and not been so hasty in turning her money over to him.

I knew he wouldn't be stupid enough to leave his laptop here. My prior experience at the marketing firm would allow me to crack open his passwords and get everything I need to get to his ass. There has to be something here that I can use. I know that I'm just overlooking it and it's staring me in my face. I swear when I find his ass I'm going to kill him whether he has money or not making me go through all this to find him. Chandelle looked across the room towards Rena as she tore into his books on the shelves looking for any clues to who he was dealing with or where he may be in New York.

"You find anything interesting Rena?" Chandelle asked breaking from perusing his desk hoping fresh eyes will see something she may have overlooked.

"No. Have you?"

"No. But I do know one thing, if there's something of importance here it's well-hidden and he didn't have any plans on coming back here. It's as if he cleaned this place out knowing someone might come in here checking up on him."

"You're probably right. There's nothing over here but some books and papers on marketing his services. Nothing that ties him to anybody. Just some flyers. He even has a flyer over here about some dinner function at a local restaurant being held tomorrow." Chandelle pulled open a desk drawer then realized Rena may have found just what they needed to find Xavier.

"Rena, did you say a dinner function as in a fund raiser? Let me see that for a minute." Rena walked towards the desk to give Chandelle the flyer she had thrown to the floor in her search.

"Girl, this isn't the time to worry about getting something to eat! What do you need it for?"

"I'm not looking for food genius! I just remembered Xavier telling me about a friend of his who wanted him to get involved in something that has to do with a fundraiser at his restaurant. Maybe he can give us some information on where we can find Xavier." Chandelle searched the flyer for a name and phone number and after finding it she grabbed the phone to quickly dial the number. Rena sat down at the desk in hopes that Chandelle found what they were looking for. After two rings she listened to the male voice that answered.

"Xavier, where the fuck have you been? I hope you are calling me with good news about having my money."

"I'm sorry but this isn't Xavier. I am looking for Brian Carver." Chandelle said hesitantly knowing she may have found who she wanted to talk to without needing Brian Carver.

"Oh. Allow me to apologize. I recognized the phone number as Xavier Barnes and I thought you may have been him on the

line. Anyway, I'm Brian Carver. How can I help you?"

Chandelle smiled knowing she got what she was looking for.

"Hi, Mr. Carver, my name is Chandelle Carter and it seems that you and I have something in common."

"Is that right? And what is that Ms. Carter"

"Please call me Chandelle. Well, it seems that we are both looking for Xavier. I was calling you because he told me that he was a friend of yours and I was hoping that you could tell me where I might find him." There was a short pause on the other line as if Brian was thinking about what he wanted to share with this mysterious person on the other line.

"You can say that we are friends. Why are you looking for Xavier and why would I tell you where he is if I do know?"

"It seems by the way you answered the phone, Xavier owes you some money and I am having the same problem. I recently gave Mr. Barnes my life savings in hopes that he could invest the money for a fast return on my money. He promised that he had an investment that would help me with some increasing hospital bills I have for my sick aunt." Chandelle hoped that using her aunts' sickness would give her the sympathy she wanted to get the information she needed to find Xavier.

"You're right. Xavier does owe me some money. But I'm sure that he explained to you Ms. Carter that investing money in the market isn't a guarantee and there is always a chance that you may lose on your investment." Brian hated telling Ms. Carter that she had to take some responsibility for her investment when he knew that Xavier used some shady friends of his to double his own investment. But he also knew that his last investment was without his permission and was now wondering how desperate or deep in debt his friend was to steal from the unknowing.

"I understand that Mr. Carver but Xavier assured me that the investment he was making on my behalf was a guarantee to double or even triple my investment. He explained that he had friends on Wall Street that from time to time help him attract clients with investments that would make money for them."

"How do you know Xavier Ms. Carter? Were the two of you lovers?"

"No not exactly but we were certainly attracted to each other. There was hope that when this deal was over we could go a little farther in our relationship and see where it took us. I didn't want to mix business with pleasure. I'm not implying that I wanted to see if he came through for me first on this investment but I was new to the island and I have yet to find a place to stay and dig my nails in." Chandelle didn't want to get into the fact that she just got out of a bad relationship and didn't feel it was necessary. At this point she figured he was either going to tell her what she needed to know or she was going to have look for another clue in his office concerning his whereabouts.

"I see. You are correct in your assumptions about me and Xavier. He does owe me some money. I'm not going to share something with you because of what he owes me but because it seems Xavier has gone too far and I'd hate to see this happen

to anybody else." Chandelle smiled and nodded to Rena letting her know they'd hit the jackpot.

"I know he's in New York but I don't know where he's staying. He's also not answering his phone. I know you probably tried to call him yourself."

A look of concern suddenly showed on Chandelle's face that Brian may not be able to help her at all. He had yet shared anything with her that she didn't already know.

"He did tell me that he had a guy named Charles Goldberg had a small firm in lower Manhattan called Goldberg and Weinstein Brokers. I don't have the number but I believe you can look it up yourself and find it. I don't know anything about any other friends you said he mentioned. Anyway, that dude was supposed to be the source of some investments he made for me. I can bet he can help you find Xavier. If there are other people involved he would be able to lead you to them since they are in the business. If you find Xavier tell him to give me a call."

Thank you so much for your help. I appreciate it. I will tell Xavier to call you. By the way, I wish you success with your fundraiser."

"Thank you Chandelle." Chandelle listened as the other line went dead. Chandelle hung up the phone and went into a daze deep in thought.

"Well? What happened Chandelle? What did he say?"

"He gave me a name and a business that Xavier is associated with."

"Well, what are we waiting for? Let's call them? This could be what we were looking for!" Chandelle sat quietly thinking.

"I don't know if we will be that lucky Rena calling this guy. First of all, if we can get him to admit that he knows Xavier, he will probably never admit that they did business together. What they were doing was illegal. His telling me anything could implicate him and charges being brought against him and his losing his license."

"So what do you suggest we do? We have to do something." Rena said beginning to get frustrated.

"I got an idea. Remember my telling you about my Uncle Donnie who lived in New York?"

"Yeah, I remember. What about him?"

"He has very important friends there. Maybe he can help us get the information we need from this guy that would lead us to Xavier. If this Charles guy is correctly implicated by someone with some pull he may come off of the info we need if there is a promise not to tell the authorities about his shady dealings."

"When are you going to call your uncle?"

"I'm going to call him right now. You use the cell and get us to New York by tomorrow morning. I can ask him to meet us somewhere so we can lay out the story. He'll instruct us on what to do from there.

∙∙∙

Xavier just finished having some dinner and laid back on his pillow drinking his Heineken and turned his remote to TNT to catch the second half of the Knicks game. Xavier checked his watch and saw that it was still early enough to call Brian. If everything failed him he knew that he never wanted to lose Brian's friendship or try to pay him what he owed. Xavier grabbed his cell not wanting Wright to know who he was calling or anything else about his personal life he didn't already know.

"Hey man. I wanted to call and touch base with you. I'm not going to make your function tonight man but we're going to hook up real soon."

"I'm shocked to hear from you man. I haven't heard from you in a couple of weeks and now you call me today. What a coincidence."

"A coincidence? I'm not following you. What is that supposed to mean?"

"I got a phone call concerning you today. I haven't heard from you and today I get two calls. That's the coincidence."

"Who called you about me?" Xavier said knowing that he and Brian didn't share the same group of friends and none of his women friends knew Brian well enough to call on his behalf.

"A woman called here earlier. Her name was Chandelle Carter. She said you were a friend of hers. You do know her right?" Brian said with a snicker in his voice.

"Yes, I know her. What did she want? What did she say?" Xavier said half relieved it wasn't the police looking for him with everything he had going on in his life lately.

"She said something about you taking her money and guaranteeing her a return on her money. She said you never called her and wanted to know if I knew how to get in contact with you."

"What did you tell her man?"

"Before I get into that, I got some questions for you my man. I'm not going to cuss your ass out cause you seem to be in more trouble than you can handle. What kind of shit are you into man?"

"Nothing too deep. I made a bad investment for Chandelle and I just didn't have the heart to tell her yet. She knew the risk. You know man that there's no sure thing to investing money. She understood the risk."

"I alluded to the same thing with her but it was funny how she mentioned that you told her about your friends in New York and how you get inside information that you share with special clients. Don't try to bullshit me Xavier. You ran that same shit to me when you first started out. It was very successful for both of us so I know she's not lying. What happened?" Xavier decided not to go around and around with Brian. He knew he couldn't deceive his best friend and he wanted to talk to someone he trusted and get some of the weight off his back.

"I wanted to get your money back man. I'm not trying to use that as an excuse 'cause I was sincerely attracted to her. The lead I got for the investment was like all the others and from the same source. It was legit. Anyway, to make a long story short, I was set up. My man from New York reminded me that he was giving me the leads to build up my practice in return for a favor I would have to give in return at a later date. My number came up on this one. I came out here and made the investment and got caught up in a scam."

"What kind of scam?" Brian said with concern in his voice.

"Charles gives out insider information then they cash in by asking you to deliver a package as the fee. Once you deliver the package, the recipient claims the package isn't correct and extorts money from you to make the situation correct so you can walk away with your life."

"They threatened your life man?"

"In so many words yes. They leave you without any choice. I guess they picked this time to collect because of the amount I invested. My past investments building your portfolio for example, were smaller amounts. They wait for you to make a large investment so they can get all that you invested plus the money you made."

"I don't get it. If they know that you are going to make money from the investment, why don't they just invest their own money?"

"I guess cause they don't want a money trail that would lead back to them. What's the difference when they know that someone else is going to buy the stock and they can take yours? This way they're clean. Who knows how many other brokers they have involved in this scam? If they have five or six other brokers involved, we're talking millions man."

"Damn Xavier. I almost feel sorry for you man. You're a smart brotha. You didn't have to do this. You should know better than anybody that there's no love in quick money schemes. So now what? How do you plan to get out of this?" Xavier thought about how he wanted to answer his question. He had Brian's sympathy and didn't want to ruin it by letting him know that he could've paid back some of which he owed without being part of the scam he was involved in.

"I met some legitimate guys who are able to help me get out of this jam. I was able to meet with them before I paid off the scam. Instead of paying the ransom to Charles I'm giving the money to them so that I have a chance to have some semblance of a normal life. I'll get a name and passport so I can get out of town." Xavier said letting his friend know that he doesn't know when he'll see him again.

"I understand. Look, I told Chandelle that you were in New York. She had already suspected that you were. I did give her Charles Goldberg's name and the company he works for. I hope that this doesn't interfere with your plans but I felt she needed to know something. It sounds to me that you'll be long gone before she can track you down anyway." Xavier sighed contemplating whether the information Brian shared would interfere with his getaway plan.

"Okay man. I understand why you did it. If she goes to Charles Goldberg there is no way that he would lead her to me. He would be placing his license and life in jeopardy. He'd have to admit that what he and I were doing was illegal. There is no way he would implicate himself. Besides, he's probably looking for me himself. I didn't pay his partner the money they were asking." *"Take care man. I hope that you can turn this shit around. When you get a chance give me a call and let me know you're okay."*

"I'll do that Brian. Brian, I swear I'll make all of this right by you. I'll get you what you're owed." Xavier could hear Brian breathing on the other side of the line then a soft click of the call disconnecting. *Damn! I was just starting to feel a little comfortable about this shit! Now I have Chandelle out here looking for me. There are about eight million people in New York. There is no way she can find me in a day or two. I hope when I get this call tomorrow, Mr. Wright will be able to tell me he has my passport and I can get the hell out of here.* Xavier picked up the remote to turn the game up hoping that watching the Knicks play basketball would drown out both his thoughts and fears.

Chapter 21

Chandelle for the first time in days felt that she was going to get her money and life back. She'd hardly slept after speaking with her uncle about the events that had turned her life upside down in the past few weeks. She explained that she needed his help with finding an individual that stole her life savings from underneath her. She was careful not to tell him her part in the scheme that was supposed to make her rich in fear that he would give her a speech about being responsible for her own doings and reaping what she sowed. He was so proud of her and all of her accomplishments with completing school with her Masters degree after all the mischievous situations she often found herself in as a child. He promised her that he would always have her back as long as she kept her nose clean. Chandelle knew she played a small part in her current situation but the worse he could do is say he wouldn't help her and she wouldn't be any worse off than she already was.

"What are you so deep in thought about Chandelle? Are you nervous about seeing your uncle?" Rena said getting Chandelle's attention.

"Yeah, I'm thinking about my uncle. He has connections girl and I know he can make this happen. I just gotta be careful about how I explain this whole thing to him. He's not going to be happy if he finds out that I gave Xavier my money knowing he was doing something illegal."

"He wouldn't understand? I can't believe that Chandelle."

"He'd be sympathetic but the stock market is a gamble and he knows I know that. He would just tell me to take the loss like the rest of the world. I've decided that I'm going to put a spin on it and tell him that Xavier didn't do as instructed with the money that was going to be invested and I got suspicious when he didn't return any of my phone calls. I'll then explain that when you and I went to his office and found his stuff gone I suspected that he probably just got ghost with my money."

"So you're gonna say he didn't do as instructed cause you didn't hear from him?"

"Damn right! If you gave someone some money and they never came back would you not think they didn't do the right thing, stole your money and disappeared?"

"You're right! I can't argue that. I saw that the stock he invested in on my behalf didn't do poorly. He didn't lose the money Rena. So why would he not return my calls? He obviously took my money and the return on the investment and ran. I'm not going to rest till I get my shit back."

"I hear you. We're getting ready to land. Your uncle is meeting us when we get off the plane?"

"Yes. He said he is going to have a driver waiting for us to take us into the city."

■■■

Xavier woke to the sound of the phone ringing on the side table next to his bed. The last thing he remembered was watching an old black and white western on the television drinking enough beers to knock him unconscious since he couldn't force himself to sleep. Noticing it was after ten in the morning from the digital clock display next to the phone, he fumbled, clumsily to answer the phone.

"Xavier, I hope I didn't wake you."

"It's okay. I usually don't sleep this late. Do you have some good news for me?"

"I wish I did. I tried to no avail to get our guy that handles passports put one together for you. He won't be available 'til this evening. The earliest I can get you out of town is tomorrow morning. But let me assure you that you are safe and if there is anything you need all you have to do is give me a call and I can take care of it for you." Xavier held his head not sure if it was the bad news that made him aware that he had a raging headache or a hangover from drinking too many beers.

"I guess if there was anything that you could do you would have handled it for me. I'll be fine with tomorrow. If you hear anything that could move it up to today no matter how late, I'd be happy to get on a late flight tonight."

"I understand your urgency. It's hard starting over and I'm sure you're ready to get on with your life. If I can make other arrangements I will handle it." Xavier hung up the phone disappointed he wouldn't be leaving today but did feel safe nonetheless. It was better than being in a hotel somewhere where he could be recognized by sheer coincidence. *I got to find out if there is something here for a headache. Then I'm going to go downstairs and make something to eat. I need to call the bank and find out exactly how much money I have left then figure out where I can run and hide out for a while. I'll take out my laptop and surf the internet and find somewhere I can live comfortably. Wright told me to let him know where I'd like to go so I need to gather a plan to make that happen. I always wanted to go to Europe but I may have to go somewhere like Mexico where I can live rather cheaply. Let me get started so I can make this happen.*

■■

Chandelle, Rena and Donnie sat in Juniors restaurant for an early lunch and to explain what happened that brought her to New York. Chandelle suggested they get something to eat rather than go to a hotel room and be let down if he decided that he couldn't help her. It was bad enough that she spent the money for airfare hoping she didn't do so in vain. She immediately reverted to her old frugal self, trying to hold on to every penny she had. The two million she gave Xavier left her nearly broke and she only had the fifty thousand that was supposed to be used to get her cousin Nico back. She needed that money to live off of and start over if she never recovered from what she'd given Xavier. Half of the fifty thousand rightfully belonged to Rena and she would never leave her girl out in the cold. Chandelle smiled brightly when she heard her uncle call her name. He always told her she had the brightest smile and she was now willing to use it to get what she wanted.

"Chandelle, tell me what brings you here and don't leave out a thing. I can't help you if you leave out anything. There are too many people in New York. It can be like looking for a needle in a haystack if you don't give me as much information as possible." Chandelle squirmed in her seat and begun telling her side of the story.

"Uncle Donnie. To sum it all up, his name is Xavier Barnes, and he's a stockbroker from St. Croix. I gave him money to invest for me so that I could have a nest egg hoping to later invest into a new business. I met him on the island. Rena and I were planning to move there and start a business. Anyway, I went home to Pittsburgh to help Rena with her mom and she and I went back to meet with Xavier and he was gone. I went to his office and noticed that he'd cleaned his place out. I got in touch with one of his friends who told me he was involved in an insider trading scheme. His connection in New York is Charles Golberg of Goldberg and Weinstien Brokers in Manhattan. That's all I know. Now I gave you the long and the short of it. Do you think you can help me?"

"I have some friends that can maybe help us. I won't make you tell me again. I believe you. I have a couple of questions but I won't get into any of that until this whole thing is over. I'm glad to see that you and your friend were trying to put money away for the future and open your business. The only thing you didn't tell me was how much money we're talking?"

Chandelle knew this question was going to come up and could possibly be the deal breaker. But she had to be truthful if there was any hope in seeing her money again.

"Two million dollars." Chandelle watched as her uncle nearly choked on the coffee he was drinking.

"Two million dollars? Where the hell did you get two million dollars? Is there something you're not telling me? Did this man invest for you earlier and earned you two million?"

"No. He had nothing to do with my savings. That money was part of a settlement I had with my previous employer, along with my 401k and all the money Rena had to her name. This was a joint venture. I swear the money isn't dirty," she lied. Donnie stared at his neice which seemed liked hours to see if she was lying. When she was a little girl he was always able to tell if she was lying. Her left eye would twitch uncontrollably giving her away. She also became very fidgety in her chair. Chandelle sat tight looking her uncle square in the eye.

"I believe you. I'm going to get you ladies a room. It's going to take the rest of the day to get us some help with this. I'm going to make some phone calls then get in touch with you later."

"Oh, thank you. Thank you! I knew you'd come through for me." Chandelle jumped from her chair and hugged her uncle then hugged Rena in relief.

"Get yourself together. I'm going to call the driver back and instruct him to take you to the Marriott in Times Square. Your luggage is still in the trunk of the car. I need to get to uptown to my office and make some calls. You don't have to stay cooped up in your room. I'll call your cell when I get some information."

■■

Xavier spent the morning on the computer researching Mexico and where he could live comfortably for a long period of time until he came up with a plan that would make him more money. He picked Mexico because he had a dear friend from college who took a job in the Foreign Services and traveled the world frequently. She used to talk about how inexpensive it was to live there but little to do in terms of a social life. That was exactly what he needed. He figured his being black would stick out like a sore thumb but he wanted to spend time alone and breathe his own air anyway. He quickly decided on living in Bosques de Las Lomas. The pictures in the ads showed mini mansions for rent for a thousand dollars a month. They were equal to a five hundred thousand- dollar home on the island. Many were five bedrooms complete with all the modern amenities like stainless steel appliances, swimming pools, extra rooms used as game-rooms and libraries. All had eight foot retaining walls surrounding them to keep families with children secure. A maid who cooks would cost an additional three hundred a month and another hundred would hire a driver. Xavier wasn't sure about the maid or driver because he wanted to stay low key. He'd wait to get down there to make that decision. He decided for the huge house so curious onlookers would believe that more than one person occupied his dwelling. Xavier called the number in the listing and made arrangements to view the property the next day. Satisfied with his choice, he called Mr. Wright to tell him what his plans were.

"Xavier, what can I do for you?"

"I made a decision where I want to go. I need a ticket to Bosques De Las Lomas in Mexico City. You may need to book the flight to Mexico City and I may have to take a bus to my destination."

"Good, I can take care of that. Everything on my end is proceeding as planned. Our guy is in town working on your passport now."

"I don't need a passport to get to Mexico." Xavier said hoping to get a flight out of town that evening.

"I didn't know that. But you will need the passport. Your drivers' license and birth certificate are no longer any good if you are trying to stay undercover. You'll need the passport to get new identification."

"I didn't think about that. You're right. Well, the earliest flight out tomorrow will be good. Do you think it's possible I can be at the airport by noon?"

"I think we can make that happen. I'll have the driver pick you up in the morning."

"I'll see you at your office."

■■

Chandelle and Rena were taking in the sights of Times Square when her phone rang. She answered quickly noticing the number belonged to her uncle updating her on what the plans would be for the following day. Chandelle ran to the opposite side of the street with Rena following her to a quiet spot so she could hear.

"Chandelle, you and your friend get ready to leave the hotel at around eleven. Get some breakfast in you cause it could be a long day. I have an appointment for us to meet a good friend of mine at his place of employment. He owes me a favor. He said he has another appointment and will be able to see us after that. He said he'd squeeze us in. He's leaving town in the early afternoon but his info is usually on point and will get us what we need."

"Okay, we'll be ready. See you then."

Chapter 22

Xavier was more than a little excited and hardly slept all. He was up at seven in the morning cooking breakfast and made a fresh cup of coffee. He sat in front of the television watching the Today show remembering his college days when the women in the dorm insisted that it was on promptly at seven every morning. Xavier hated the show back then but began to appreciate its variety of topics from sports and politics to fashion and cooking. He couldn't enjoy the show in St. Croix because none of the networks carried the show. Xavier waited for the phone to ring announcing what time the driver would arrive to pick him up. Xavier checked his luggage for the third time to make sure that he wasn't forgetting anything. He didn't want to leave the bedroom in fear that he might miss the call. An hour passed and the phone rang at nine sharp.

"Good morning, Xavier. Your car will arrive at ten thirty to pick you up. We will tie up any loose ends and you will be on your way to the airport."

"Thanks. I'll be ready." Xavier felt like a child on Christmas morning. He finally felt as if his nightmare was coming to an end." He checked his watch and saw he had an hour to kill before his ride arrived. Xavier leaned back in his chair and counted the minutes as they passed.

■■■

Chandelle and Rena showered early in the morning and threw on jeans and t-shirts to have breakfast in the hotel restaurant. Chandelle explained to Rena how important their meeting was going to be with her uncles' connection. She let Rena know that they had an eleven o'clock meeting and they should dress as professional as possible to impress her uncle and his friend. She let her know that they weren't dealing with street thugs therefore, they should look like they mean business. Chandelle smoothed her curly bob to lay straight and framed her face with a three inch bang. She decided on a navy blue Micheal Kors suit with a white sheer but tasteful camisole. She decided against pantyhose because it was expected to be a warm day and pantyhose made her itch. She finished her outfit with four inch blue sling backs. Rena followed Chandelle's lead and wore a black pants suit with a heather grey cami by Donna Karan. She completed her outfit with a pair of Ralph Lauren pumps. She decided against fussing with her hair. She chose to pull it back in a tight ponytail and sported a French knot. Both were pleased with their outfits and knew they were sure to please anyone who laid eyes on them.

"Chandelle, I'm ready are you? The car will be here any minute. It's ten and it's going to take time to get where we're going. Did he tell you where we're going?"

"I'm ready. He didn't say but I'm not worried about it. I'm sure we will have enough time to get where we are going. Grab your luggage. I have mine. We might as well wait in the lobby 'til he gets here."

•••

Xavier was escorted to the third floor office where he previously met Mr. Wright. Xavier had a seat and waited until Alexander came in to give him the necessary paperwork to leave town. Xavier checked his watch and saw that it was ten forty-five and he planned to be at the airport by noon. He was already cutting it close and Mr. Wright had yet to show up. Suddenly, the door opened and Mr. Wright came into the office offering his apologies for being late.

"I'm so sorry to keep you waiting Xavier. Doug will be here any minute but we can get most of this transaction done before he gets here. I quoted you a fee of two hundred thousand. Minus my fee of a hundred and fifty thousand and fifty thousand to Doug for your passport will take care of the payments. You can write me a separate check for three hundred for the price of your air fare. On second thought, I'm feeling generous, forget about the three hundred. Sign the bottom of the cashiers' check. The only thing left is to wait for Doug to bring your passport."

"What time is the plane?"

"I know I told you noon. I didn't think you'd make it so I changed your reservations for three. I'll drop you off at the airport as soon as he arrives." Alexander watched as Xavier signed the cashier checks. Wright picked up his check and placed it inside suit jacket.

"Xavier, make yourself comfortable. I know it's early but if you want to make yourself a drink you're welcome to it. I have a previous engagement at eleven and they'll be arriving momentarily. I'm meeting them downstairs so I will be able to see when Doug enters the bank. As soon as he arrives I'll bring him to you so that you can get to the airport on time." Xavier shook his head in agreement but couldn't shake the nervousness that loomed in the base of his stomach. He couldn't wait to have his passport in hand so he could get to the airport.

■■

Chandelle, Rena and Donnie pulled up to the Harlem National Bank for their appointment. Chandelle quizzically looked at the building and wondered why they were meeting their connection at a bank.

"Uncle Donnie, what are we doing here? This is a weird place to meet your connection."

"This is his place of business. I had to get special permission to bring you here. He is a very good friend of mines but there's a code that everyone obeys. One of them is that you don't bring personal business to where you make your money. I let him know what you told me and he agreed that time was limited. He's leaving town so he agreed to allow you to come. He knows you're my niece. Just listen closely and follow my lead. Obey the rules I gave you. Don't talk too much. Only ask the questions he asks of you okay? He's a good guy but he thinks women are emotional and usually doesn't work with them outside the banking business. Remember when I was telling you about the Black Mafia? Well, he and his brothers are the head of that organization. So he means business." Rena pulled on Chandelle's jacket to whisper in her ear.

"Girl, I know this is your family and all, but the Black Mafia? This is some deep shit. I'm scared as hell! This isn't anything like those street thugs in the streets. These people here can not only kill your family but they will take out any babies you might be even thinking about having."

"Calm down girl. My uncle got this. Just follow the rules. Don't say shit and we'll be fine."

The three of them exited the car and went inside and took the first available seats in the waiting area. A tall blonde in her early thirties walked towards them stating that Mr. Wright was available for their eleven o'clock meeting and that they should follow her. Donnie walked behind the blonde with Chandelle and Rena following behind him. They were escorted to the bank managers' office and greeted at the door by Mr. Wright. Chandelle watched as he and her uncle exchanged pleasantries.

"What's going on man? It was nice hearing from you. How's the wife?"

"She's good and yours?"

"Lil is doing well. We need to get together outside of business. I never see any of my good friends."

"I hear you. Ever since I was awarded that huge contract to rebuild Harlem, I never get a chance to see anyone."

"I was able to take care of your niece's situation. In fact, I had that situation taken care of five minutes after you phoned." Donnie looked in amazement at what his friend was saying. He knew how he worked and got things done but never did he think he would take care of his situation so quickly. It took everything Chandelle had in her not to scream out in joy and ask questions on how she could get her money back. Rena gripped harder on her armchair till the white showed through her knuckles. Mr. Wright's revelation confirmed just how dangerous she believed him to be. She figured right then and there her life was going to be short lived for a favor she'd never be able to return.

"Are you kidding me man? How did you get to him so quickly?"

"He kinda fell into my lap by accident. Turns out he was being extorted of some money he made in an investment. The people he was dealing with were feeding him inside information only for him to make a payment for the information down the road. Those same individuals wanted a million dollar payment for his services. He came to the bank to get a wire transfer from his bank in the island to make the payment. When customers ask for the kind of money they are usually doing something illegal, being blackmailed or something similar. So I offered him my services. I offered to give him an apartment to stay in 'til I provided him with the papers he needed to leave the country." Donnie looked at Chandelle as if he was reading her mind to get the information she wanted.

"So how did you handle it?"

"Well, I brought him to the bank. I knew you would be here and I arranged for him to come here to pick up his passport. I took my fees for the services I provided of course. I took the liberty to clean out his account in the islands so that you could recoup your money. I can give you the bank draft now and you can leave out the back door. You won't get the full two million but considering you had nothing when you got here a million and a half is nothing to cry about." Chandelle began to cry happy that she was going to move on in life as she and Rena had planned. She wasn't moving to St. Croix but anywhere was okay with her as long as she wasn't broke.

"Are you satisfied Donnie?" Donnie looked at Chandelle and was surprised to see her shake her head no. Mr. Wright for the first time during the meeting gave Chandelle his attention and spoke.

"What can I do for you dear? I'm going to assume that you are Chandelle?"

"Yes, I'm Chandelle. Thank you so much for your help but I do have one request. Can I please talk to him? I need to ask him why. I want him to know that he hasn't won and he will think twice before fucking someone else around." Alexander thought for a minute and picked up the receiver of the phone. He dialed a number then stated that he was in need of security at the branch manager's office. Chandelle stirred in her chair frightened that she may have asked the impossible and was being escorted off the premises. The office door opened to beautiful bald six foot figure that read business across his face.

"Raul, Xavier is upstairs in my office. He seems comfortable with you. Go and assure him that I will be there shortly." Raul left as quietly as he entered and headed towards the elevator.

"Chandelle, I'm going to give you your wish. You will have to follow a few rules though while you are in my office. You are free to say whatever you please. I do not want you to go near him and do any bodily harm. This is my place of business and I don't want to alarm any customers we have in the lobby. Do you understand?"

"Yes, thank you. I promise. I'll keep my hands to myself." Chandelle smiled and rose from her chair. She hugged her uncle whispering thank you in his ear. She then grabbed Rena's hand and together they walked out the office behind Mr. Wright and Donnie towards the elevator.

Xavier turned around when he heard the office door open and smiled when he saw Alexander Wright come through the door. Alexander took a seat behind his desk. Xavier's heart nearly stopped when he saw Chandelle walk in behind a gentlemen he never saw before with another unknown woman in tow.

"What is this? What's going on?" Xavier yelled wanting someone to answer his question. Chandelle stood beside her uncle and spoke first.

"You almost got away with this. You never know who knows who huh? I believed in you Xavier. I really did. But you had to get greedy and steal my money. Well guess what? I got every dime. You ain't get shit. Your bank account has been wiped out. How does it feel? You're lucky that you are being protected in this office by Mr. Wright because if we were in the streets, I swear I would've killed your ass. But believe this, if I ever see you again in this lifetime you won't be so lucky." Chandelle said what was on her mind and was finally at peace with herself. She headed to the door when she heard Xavier scream,

"Bitch you took my money? How the fuck am I supposed to live now?" Chandelle turned and laughed aloud saying,

"You fucked with the wrong bitch Xavier! Your problem is for you to figure out. Xavier stood from his chair to take a leap towards Chandelle but was held back by Raul, Mr. Wright's driver. Thinking quickly, Xavier remembered that Raul carried a gun under his suit jacket. Xavier reached under Raul's jacket and pulled the gun out and aimed it at Chandelle. Xavier pulled back the hammer and then a loud gunshot was heard and blood shot across the room as Chandelle collapsed to the floor. Xavier then dropped the gun realizing what he did. A loud scream was heard as Rena fell to the floor in tears agonizing over Chandelle's fate.

"No! Chandelle! Please open your eyes! Don't leave me now!" Rena cried. Alexander Wright ran from behind his desk and yelled for Raul to take her and Donnie down the back steps.

"Get her to my private room then come back to my office! Now!" Raul picked Chandelle off of the floor away from Rena's reaching arms. Mr. Wright snatched the gun from the blood soaked carpet and asked that Rena and Donnie follow Raul down the back steps to his private quarters. The office door opened and Alexander's secretary and bodyguard Maxwell came into the room.

"Mr. Wright are you okay?" The blonde asked.

"I'm fine. Get someone to clean up this mess and run interference in the lobby for any concerned customers. The blonde woman exited as fast as she entered. Maxwell remained by Mr. Wrights side awaiting his orders.

"Xavier, you fucked up. I was going to allow you to leave here with your life. You would've been broke but you would've had your life. I believe you just made a stupid mistake trusting Charles but it would be a lesson learned. Now you have to pay for what you done.

"Maxwell, take this gentlemen down the back entrance and take care of him. Dump his body with all the others."

"Mr. Wright please! I didn't mean to shoot her. I lost my mind. Please…" Rena appeared from behind the door leading to the back stairs. She quickly grabbed the gun from the bodyguards hand and held it to Xavier's head. A loud echoing shot fired from the gun and Rena watched as his lifeless body fell to the floor.

"I guess you make body number four mother fucker." Rena returned the gun to Maxwell then slowly walked down the back steps.

Made in the USA
Lexington, KY
15 May 2013